M000110347

Shield of Honor

Danney Clark

Copyright © 2012 Danney Clark

All rights reserved.

Preface

It is important for me to let the reader know this is fiction. The 9/11
events, while based on fact, could never, as described, do justice to the
full and complete story of the event. September 11, 2001, is significant to
America and the world and was therefore chosen specifically as another
window into Cady Miller's remarkable life. It is my hope and prayer that
the reader will find personal value in these books far beyond the
competency of their writer. May God be honored as the reader realizes
that nothing happens independent of God's power.

One

Amid the explosions and aerial displays that marked our nation's Independence Day, he heard a yell followed by a louder and sharper report that was closely followed by a second and third. Cady, in his blue uniform with Kevlar vest and duty belt, was lifted off his feet by the impact and fell fifteen feet from the pier into the East River. As he settled below the water's dark surface, his mind continued to register the colors of the fireworks in the sky overhead. *Yea, though I walk through the valley of the shadow ...,* drifted through his mind like smoke. The water was cold, less than sixty degrees, there under the pier even though the summer sun had warmed its surface during the day. Taking stock of the situation, he was aware that the force of two of the three bullets had been absorbed by the vest, knocking out his breath and possibly breaking a couple of ribs. The third, however, had entered where the vest was cut out to allow arm movement. His mind registered that there had been two shooters. The first one had hit him squarely in the chest and the second from the side at an angle. It was that bullet that caused the pain.

His left arm burned, indicating it had been hit before the round followed around his back and ricocheted off his scapula. The weight of his duty belt took him deeper and deeper into the river and farther and farther from shore. *Think before you act. Don't breathe, don't struggle,* his trained mind told him as he unbuttoned his belt with his gun still in it. He felt it drop away below him as he loosened the Velcro that held his vest around him. Both arms and legs worked hard as he fought toward the surface. His teeth clinched tightly as he overrode his natural desire to breathe while alarms were going off in a brain that he was starving of oxygen.

As his head broke the water's surface he half expected to hear the shots that would take his life. They did not come. Gasping for air and struggling in the current, he understood why. The pier was several hundred yards upstream from him. The darkness and distance prevented him from being seen. Three figures stood under the yellow glow of the light on the pier looking down where he had fallen, ready should he resurface.

He was part of a special task force brought together in an attempt to secure access from the river to those with the intent to smuggle explosives, guns, drugs and contraband into New York. As a veteran officer, having worked with military and the FBI, he had the special skills desired when attempting to combat terrorism. He could have used his rank to ride a desk and serve only in a supervisory capacity rather than putting his feet on the ground, but he chose to lead from the front. Skills unique to him came from many hours of study and hard work under the tutelage of some of the best America could offer. He was one of very few who had completed SEALS training, spent time in Langley while not on their payroll, and studied criminal psychology with a room full of Mensa guys at Quantico.

There had been three in his unit when they stopped to investigate a forty-foot fishing boat that was tied at a pier reserved for pleasure craft.

It appeared to be a routine patrol with no indications of anyone on board until the moment Cady watched his partner's head explode. Before he could draw his weapon he had been hit from the darkness also. The third man on the team, John Day, had been waiting at the car to relay their report. Cady hoped he had escaped and had been able to call for backup.

It was nontypical that smugglers would assassinate two officers without provocation even in New York. Apparent to Cady that his assailants were willing to take the offensive to the streets made them all the more dangerous. He was beginning to shiver, the cold water was taking its toll and pushing him toward the point of no return as his core temperature dropped. He continued to float rather than to swim toward a man-made jetty ahead that reached out to him. Overhead a myriad of colors and lights continued to interrupt the night sky as the celebration continued.

~

Cady Miller, having served twenty-five years in law enforcement, first in Idaho as a county sheriff and now ten in New York City, was approaching fifty at an alarming rate. Although he was still trim and athletic, his hair showed gray at his temples. His wife, Shawna, educated and beautiful, ten years his junior, still held the exuberance of youth. She had long black hair and a radiant smile. Moving east had, at first, been difficult for Shawna. She knew no one and had no relatives. She was born on a Blackfoot Indian reservation in Idaho where her family ties went back generations. Although she was educated, holding a degree in social services with another in nursing, she had always worked from home. Faith, their oldest, and her twin sisters were young children when they arrived in the Big Apple. They missed the mountains, trees, and the fresh smell of the outdoors. They gradually learned to enjoy the city for what it was and not want for what it lacked.

John, his first partner and best friend, was nearing retirement. He had no desire to leave the streets or climb the ladder to detective. Cady took several seconds to pray to God for John's safety. It had been John who had explained salvation to Cady in such a way as he could understand and believe in it. It was also John and his wife, Helen, who had invited them to their church for the first time and later introduced them to Pastor Orville Ricks and his wife, Sarah. Cady knew that, live or die, he would see John again someday while walking with the Lord. Helen and John had no children, having adopted Cady's as their own while assuming the titles of aunt and uncle.

~

The jetty was fast approaching, and the strong current was trying to force Cady around and away from it. He had saved his energy for this moment knowing he had only one chance to break through the fast moving water and into the slack water beyond it. He swam hard, taking strong strokes, while refusing to panic as his strength began to wane. On the jetty he could see people seated and facing away from him. They were watching the fireworks from lawn chairs, unknowing of his desperate situation. Rather than try to scream above the noise and wasting time and energy, he concentrated on keeping a steady pace. It seemed he was destined to be washed around the protrusion and downstream. At the last second the water released its grip, and he found himself in the backwater making real headway toward land.

Exhausted, he pulled himself out of the water and rested on the sand and rocks. A child saw him and announced his presence to his parents. At first it seemed they might ignore him, not wanting to get involved, in the habit of the East Coasters. But soon, seeing his uniform and badge, they swarmed over to help him. Wrapped in blankets and using a borrowed cell phone, he called his precinct. He described the event and gave his location. He was told that John too had been shot after having been able to report the earlier gunshots. His condition was unknown, but he was alive and in hospital care. Cady repeated his earlier prayer adding thanks to his petition. It the distance he could hear sirens and see lights approaching. He closed his eyes and gave up his struggle to stay awake.

Cady awakened hours later one floor below his friend John, who had just come out of surgery and into ICU. As he opened his eyes, Shawna, his daughters, and several of his brothers in blue greeted him with worried smiles. He understood that he had just come from surgery where they had treated his wound and removed a bullet. Heating pads felt heavy on him as they attempted to artificially restore his body temperature by pumping hot liquid through them.

"John is going to make it," Shawna whispered, leaning close to his ear. "Helen is with him now."

During the ensuing days he and John were debriefed by the detectives in their own squad, the FBI, and a special squad from the CIA. As he became more alert he began to piece parts of the puzzle together suspecting that there was suspicion of more than drug smuggling involved in their assault. Neither he nor John were able to make the funeral of their fallen comrade and left their families instead to represent them.

~

By the first of August he was back, assigned to light duty and a desk. John had been released to convalesce at home under the loving care of his wife. He had suffered a collapsed lung and broken collarbone. The bullet had entered at an angle, missing vital organs but doing considerable internal damage. The jury was still out concerning his ability to return to duty. Cady visited him daily, brainstorming and going over the evidence in an attempt to find a lead to the shooters. The guns were Israeli made 10 mm weapons, military grade, probably Uzis. Fingerprints on the casings came up "no match found" in the FBI database. Ballistics also showed nothing when compared with other incidents on record.

The CIA and FBI were, unknown to most, receiving intel that pointed to a domestic attack by the Taliban or like radical groups. Leads were followed up but not shared well, each agency struggling to maintain the integrity of their own turf. Local law enforcement was of course not privy to most of the incoming intelligence and was left in the dark. Because of his place in the special unit and because he was actively involved in the investigation, Cady could access more than most. He pieced together several probable scenarios and passed them up the line where they got little consideration. The thoughts of a street cop didn't carry much weight among the intelligence community.

Behind the scenes there was a plethora of intel being intercepted and evaluated by the NSA, CIA and FBI. Smart money bet that the amount of recent activity indicated a significant likelihood of a real and imminent threat to American security. It was the little guys in each agency who seemed to see the emerging picture, not those in a position to take action. Somewhere in each the chain of command dismissed or downplayed the facts and probabilities they represented to their superiors allowing inaction to prevail.

On the tenth of August a probable match for the fishing boat turned up. The boat had been abandoned in Maryland where it had been tied up and unnoticed for several weeks. The FBI went over it finding many unidentifiable fingerprints and a single shell casing matching those from the scene. Trace evidence gave likelihood to the theory that weapons or explosives were the cargo, which were now removed from the deck. Dogs and sniffers found evidence of their presence but little more. It was July 6 when the owner of the boat reported it stolen.

~

Shawna worked three days a week as a volunteer nurse in a free clinic where she helped provide medical advice and assistance to the poor. She also worked two days a week with social services as a counselor and adviser. She specialized in teens, unwed mothers, and domestic abuse cases. Her desire was to serve and give to others from the gifts she had been given. She and Sarah Ricks, their pastor's wife, spent many hours counseling teens about options other than abortion, while witnessing to them. Many had turned over their burdens to Christ as a result. Some of the young men and women returned to visit in later years having found their way out of the lives they had once lived.

Shawna looked at each of her charges as special, often repeating, "Only God knows where He buried the gold." In her optimism she saw each with the potential to change the world using God's power.

~

Cady and Shawna lived out of the downtown area, choosing to commute rather than live among the hordes. Their time spent in the West helped them choose a small, run down, but comfortable home in a little town north and east of the city, almost to the Connecticut border. The acreage had once been a family farm, still having several outbuildings and a horse pasture. Although they could not have afforded it under normal circumstances, a member of Orville's church was more interested in the character of her buyers than in their money when the time came for her to sell. Until her death several years later, they had treated her as family and often invited her back home to join them for extended visits. The Miller children had always referred to her as their grandma when they were young.

Faith, Hope and Charity found joy in learning to ride and care for the two mares that Cady rescued. While the outside of the house looked much the same, Cady used his wood working skills to remake the inside one room at a time. John, Orville and others would sometimes drop by, making their first stop at the old barn where the tools were housed. Often they would bring a project with them, other times they would stay, helping Cady finish one. By using Cady's shop, several of the men had refurbished the old church where Orville served, making improvements where budgets would not have otherwise allowed.

~

Tuesday was the twentieth and officially John's last day on the job. He'd been forced by medical conditions and age to honor his wife's wishes to retire. Although looking fit, it was easy to see the hesitation in his stride, the lack of vitality in his eyes, and the creases pain had left in his face. The chief and the entire precinct turned out for the occasion honoring him with an adequate pension and the keys to a new RV from his fellow officers. It made it all the way to Cady's backyard on its shakedown trip. He and Helen stayed there for three days before joining the AAA and heading west to see the country together. Cady missed his old friend almost immediately, knowing they'd never share the closeness they had felt as officers.

The call came, only hours later. It was Helen calling from the doctor's office in a small town. John had had a heart attack. The old country doctor, Adrian Smith or "Smitty" to his friends, admitted him in the local hospital for evaluation. Being only a short drive, Cady and Shawna arrived in forty-five minutes and found Helen in tears. They first prayed together and then went to his room. Finding him on oxygen with monitors attached, he looked old and small to Cady.

Shawna quickly read the monitor and the notes scribbled by the attending before interpreting them to Helen and Cady. "Mild, no probable heart damage, decreased heart function indicative of insufficient blood flow to the heart."

Smitty arrived a few minutes later, having stopped to confer at the nurse' s station before entering the room. "Looks like a clogged artery. The tests may show the extent and number. We'll inject dye and have a look in a few minutes. The results will give us a direction to go," he said. He patted Helen's hand. "Don't worry, give it to God. Best case scenario we can install a stint and he'll be up and about in two days. Worst case he'll need a bypass that will require longer for recovery."

Helen attempted a smile, but failed.

Smitty continued, "Are you up to giving me a little medical history on him? I see signs of recent scarring to his chest."

Helen attempted to answer his questions, often turning to her friends for affirmation.

Finally Shawna walked him through the recent events speaking in concise medical terms.

"Makes sense," Smitty said. "The trauma, decreased lung function, and stress came together to form the "perfect storm." He has likely had blockage for sometime that is just now showing up in the picture as an MI. I can almost call it fortuitous that it happened now rather than years down the road. I should have no trouble tying this to the recent event that happened on the job. It should increase and lengthen his benefits."

Two

In their early years as teens, Cady and his sister, Kate, had been orphaned when both parents died in an automobile crash. They had lived on a small farm near Vale, Oregon, quite happily until the night that several cattle had breached a fence and attempted to cross the roadway in the darkness. Coming around a curve while returning from a Bible study meeting in town, the vehicle struck the animals at highway speed. Both children in the back seat were buckled in and survived without injuries. Both parents died of their injuries at the scene before emergency crews could arrive. Cady, nearly 18, was a senior in high school with Kate only a freshman. At his birthday he was granted custody of his sister, and he worked to support them while continuing to live on the farm. Their parents' meager life insurance had been sufficient only to give them a clear title to the property with nothing left over. For three years they struggled, both working, cleaving together with no living relatives. Their church family was able to give them spiritual and emotional support but only meager financial aid. Shortly after Kate's graduation the insurance company representing the owner of the cattle settled with them allowing both to attend college. She attended medical school in Portland. Once it became clear that neither of them had the desire to farm, Cady sold the farm and moved to the neighboring state of Idaho.

Kate married Stephan, a missionary, while she was still in school. Stephan's father had been a pastor in a suburb of Portland. As a young man, Stephan made his first mission trip in 1957. His heart was changed on this trip and his commitment became a lifetime one. Stephan and Kate had only been together a short time before being blessed with a son, Benjamin. Kate became an accomplished medical doctor and specialized in the diseases most often found in Third World countries but no longer a threat in North America. The young family traveled together all over the world. They sought and received support sufficient to make Stephan's commitment a career. They first went to South America and then to Africa. When Ben was five, his father contracted AIDS from a needle stick while in a small village in Rwanda. He died several years later of the disease. Kate returned with Ben to the states. She lived in Florida and continued to minister to immigrants, illegal immigrants and the homeless.

Ben, now approaching thirty, is married and has two children. They also live in Florida, as Ben prefers to stay near his mom. Ben's wife, Phyllis or Phil as he calls her, is a stay-at-home mother who chooses to make her family her career. Ben served in the Gulf War as an Air Force fighter pilot before his discharge. He is now a first officer with United Airlines.

~

Meanwhile Cady settled in the small eastern Idaho town of Blackfoot where he was hired as a city cop, one of five. As he gained experience and knowledge, he applied for and was hired as a deputy county sheriff. As a deputy he often worked with the Indian reservation's law enforcement on incidents both on and off the reservation. Cady was honest, affable and showed concern for both victims and perps and gained the respect of the community in the process.

Life in small town Idaho was far from exciting, so it made the newspaper when the local deputy had fallen on the ice at a traffic stop and broken his arm. Because he was near the reservation he was transported to their infirmary rather than many miles to town. That is where he met Shawna, a lovely Indian woman, fresh out of nursing school and eager to serve her community. He found himself making excuse often to return to the reservation hoping to see her. When it became evident that she shared an interest as well, he asked her to dinner and a drive-in movie. In weeks they fell in love. At the end of a year he asked her father for her hand in marriage. They were married July 4, 1986, in a small church on the reservation. In less than a year, their daughter, Faith, was born, followed a year later by the twins, Hope and Charity. October 1991 found them in New York City, strangers in a strange place, both curious of what had drawn them there, but eager to embrace God's plan.

Faith Miller was four years old and her sisters three when they left rural Idaho and arrived in New York. They had never seen a building over two stories in height except in pictures and never had flown on a plane. In the beginning it was like living a fairytale, everything new and oversized. But soon they tasted the soot of pollution in the air, and noticed that everyone was a stranger as hardly anyone made eye contact or smiled.

When they were in elementary school, schoolmates talked and acted like they were performing for their peers, which seemed unnatural and ingenuous. Their only safe harbor had been their family, and they began to withdraw into themselves. Shawna had been the first to notice the subtle changes. They smiled less, became more serious and protective of each other, and failed to joke and kid around. It seemed they had lost their innocence being forced to adopt the attitudes of the other children.

Cady was busy learning his new responsibilities at work and acclimating to the new turf, and was less sensitive to the changes. Shawna took him aside for a heart to heart, having watched their treasures change daily. They lived in the city in a rented apartment a short drive from the precinct. This allowed for no interaction out of doors. They tried but found the parks inhabited by drug dealers and perverts. Their new neighbors had no desire to know the new tenants socially, effectively isolating them from making friends.

Shawna had been in tears, Cady remembered as he recalled the time.

While she wanted to support her husband's decisions they were rapidly unraveling as a family.

Cady asked for and received a few days personal leave after explaining the situation to both his partner and commanding officer. John, his partner, had gone home and discussed the matter with his wife. They invited the Millers to their home for dinner. Shawna and Helen bonded immediately and the children for the first time since their arrival had met genuine people, people you could trust and understand. John recommended they look outside the urban area for housing, making a point to recommend areas more suited to their previous experience. Ironically, New York state had a great deal of land remaining undeveloped and pristine that did not suit the fast pace lifestyle of the mainstream populace.

As they drove, leaving the towering buildings behind, Cady could feel the tension in the car ease. Trees, grass and small villages came and went with an occasional farm animal to be seen as they passed. His daughters began to laugh and tease each other in the back seat, a sound that had been absent in their apartment. Shawna smiled when she tongue-in-cheek cautioned them to quiet down or be disciplined.

After several hours and many miles, they stopped in a small town in Franklin township to eat lunch, excited that there were no taxis or high rise buildings. They took time to walk the streets and enjoy the beauty of the fall colors brought on by the pending winter. Inside a realtors office an efficient secretary greeted them explaining that the realtor was at lunch. She did, however, give them access to multiple listings in the general area. The bubble burst immediately as they saw the prices that were far out of their reach. The were quick to realize that they were not the only ones wanting to escape the city life while still wanting the wages and benefits it provided. Wealthy people inhabited the area while continuing to enjoy careers in the city. Grateful they did not have to explain their situation to the realtor they left, returning to the city disappointed.

Back on the job, John discreetly inquired about their trip, nodding as Cady explained what had transpired. After their shift John asked Cady point blank about his spiritual life. It felt uncomfortable for only a moment before Cady confessed his belief in God, recounted his church attendance as a child, and commented on how the church had helped he and Kate after their parents died. John invited Cady and his family to join them at worship the coming Sunday.

That evening over dinner Cady asked the family to consider the offer and said that such a thing required a unanimous vote. He sat silently and waited while the four discussed it in front of him. The vote fell in favor, but there was a stipulation that the agreement was for the initial visit only. Cady agreed and accepted John's offer the next morning while in the patrol car.

The building had presumably been built in the 19th century. It occupied the same real estate for a hundred years while the city grew up around it. Although not at all presumptuous, Cady guessed that the land value would now be in the millions while the structure remained unremarkable. It had just enough parking for its congregation, as most walked or used taxis. This was an unheard of luxury. During the week, the rented parking spaces produced income, which went to the street ministry of the church that likely surpassed all income from other sources.

Remarkably, inside the church was not unlike other small churches that the Millers had attended back home, unpretentious but well appointed and maintained. Cady guessed seating capacity at three to four hundred. There were less than half that amount when they arrived with John and Helen. The pastor, Orville Ricks, was in conversation with others when they entered, but came right over to welcome them. They had only talked but a minute when a pretty, middle-aged woman joined him, his wife, Sarah. Her gaze went right to the children where she immediately began a conversation with the girls, leaving Orville to continue with the adults. Within minutes she was leading them away by the hand to show them around the parts of the church reserved for the youth group. When they returned, they were joined by two young girls about Faith's age. The five of them were busily visiting like old friends.

Sarah turned to Shawna and Cady, apologizing for her absence, "I am sorry for taking liberties with your daughters. I wanted so badly to have them meet a couple of friends before service begins. It is so difficult for children to integrate if they don't do it right away. They always seem to feel like outsiders."

Shawna took the lead, "You are so right, and thank you for making that effort. They have been so lonely since we moved to the city, I've seldom seen them smile recently or chat like they are now."

Looking over at her daughters she had to smile at the transformation.

The pianist began playing background music, which was a warning that time had neared for Orville to assume the pulpit. He excused himself, shaking hands and giving greetings as he walked forward, while Sarah took a seat beside Shawna. John and Helen were seated to Cady's left with Shawna and Sarah on his right. The children, who continued to visit and giggle, assumed seats behind them. This church retained traditional pews still having hymnals in racks along their backs. As a small choir began to sing they were brought to their feet and joined in the worship. Cady felt relieved to have the hymnal to refresh his memory of words long forgotten.

The service included two songs before an elder stood to make the congregation aware of current events including births, deaths, and changes of circumstance going on among them. He made special notice of those who had asked for prayer during the week before allowing the people to bow their heads and pray privately for several minutes. Cady found himself falling into a familiar but not recently practiced conversation with his Lord Jesus. He began, as he usually did, by acknowledging his blessings before moving on. He asked for help and guidance in areas of his life needing direction and finally prayed for protection for those in harm's way, including his brothers in blue. When he looked up it was right into Shawna's dark eyes that were filled with emotion and love, tears rimming them while threatening to overflow down her coppery cheeks.

Orville resumed control of the service by announcing that those children who desired could slip quietly away to Sunday school service. Faith and her sisters stood with her new friends waiting for permission before scampering off. As is often the way when dealing with God, the sermon seemed "laser guided" right into Cady's heart. Both Cady and Shawna felt that the pastor had some special knowledge as he spoke, of the conflicts they were enduring at this very time. It occurred to Cady for a moment that maybe John had spoken to him aforehand. He summarily dismissed the idea knowing he had not shared their situation in great detail and that John was not one to gossip.

Following the service the family seemed unwilling to return right away to their routines, hesitant to leave their newly found friends. When John asked them to stay on for the potluck, Shawna nodded her approval then looked to Cady for affirmation. The girls were delighted as well since they had met several others in Sunday school and were eager to know them better.

~

On Monday, when the girls left for school, Cady and Shawna prayed together before he left for the precinct. He took note that her prayers seemed deeper and more genuine than he had heard in a while, his own also more meaningful. With the senior man, John, driving they handled a 10-16 then relocated their 10-20 to a coffee shop where they watched the morning traffic on both street and crowded sidewalks.

John carefully broached the taboo subject. "Cady, are you and your family Christians?"

There was a long pregnant pause before Cady answered, "Yes, we believe in God and did go to church regularly back home, but haven't since moving east."

"Let me rephrase the question a little," John continued. "Are you saved? Have you asked Jesus into your life?"

At this Cady was perplexed and said, "We may not go to church as much as we should, but we do believe in God. What more is there?"

John smiled knowingly. "Only one thing, my friend, the most important one, repentance for your sin, accepting Jesus as your Lord and Savior by asking Him into your life, then giving Him control of it."

Cady was slightly irritated that John seemed to think that their lifestyle didn't qualify them as Christians. As he began to take offense, something told him to close his mouth and open his ears. So he waited for John to continue. But John did not. Instead a squawk came on their radio sending them to a traffic accident a few blocks away.

Two of the 20,000 taxis in New York had tried to occupy the same space at the same time, both relying on their horns to see them safely through. It had not worked. Traffic was backed up for blocks when they arrived at the intersection during morning commuter rush. Cady did crowd control and directed traffic while John took the report and issued tickets. One vehicle was disabled and the other returned to service with his fare on board. It took the tow truck nearly two hours to wind its way through traffic to the scene, finally allowing traffic flow to resume.

They took lunch in a small bistro in the precinct that was owned by an Italian immigrant couple from the neighborhood. They ate outside under the canopy in the crisp autumn air while staying close to their cruiser. They often made token bets between themselves whether they would have a chance to eat or be interrupted and called to service. Today they were fortunate. They each enjoyed a meatball sub with lots of marinara sauce and grated cheese. They laughed together then changed the bet to who would soil their uniform with sauce first. The rest of the day was routinely uneventful.

Back in the precinct they filed their reports and prepared to return home before Cady asked, "Aren't you going to tell me why you think I don't qualify as a Christian?"

John smiled and said quietly, "If I were the judge you'd be my first choice, however I am not, and there is only one road that leads to salvation." He continued, "Speak with Shawna, then if you are still interested in listening to me, let's spend an evening together visiting."

That evening at home while the girls fought their way through homework, Cady brought up the subject, speaking defensively to Shawna, "John doesn't think we are Christians. What do you think of that?"

Shawna hesitated before answering, "Did he say that?"

"No, not in those exact words but that's what he implied."

"That doesn't sound like John," Shawna answered. "What exactly did he say?"

"That there is only one way to get to heaven and that going to church, believing in God, and doing our best in not enough."

Shawna smiled, "Sounds about right to me. That's what I learned as a young girl on the reservation. Didn't you tell me you were a Christian when we first met?"

"Yes, and I am – aren't I?" Cady asked then wondered at what he had missed.

"God knows, I don't," she said. "No one but He can answer that question. In my personal experience though, if you have to ask you probably aren't."

Cady could feel himself getting angry and feeling judged. He even knew she had worded her answer carefully as to not seem judgmental. "So exactly what are you saying?" Cady asked, his voice rising.

"I'm saying that we should take him up on his offer and listen to what he has to say. Remember he is your friend," Shawna said softly.

Cady was feeling "double teamed" and withdrew into himself, closed down the conversation, and turned on the television. Wisely Shawna let the matter drop and joined him on the couch.

Long into the night Cady laid awake wording and rewording his arguments as his mind prepared for confrontation.

~

Wednesday morning came finally with light rain blowing in from the Atlantic and low overcast clouds adding to the grayness of the day. As they checked in, got their briefing, and accepted their assignments, Cady noticed John seemed ill at ease.

During their ten o'clock coffee break Cady broke the ice. Feeling superior and suspecting John knew he had messed up, he asked, "So John, what's bothering you this morning? Not feeling well?"

John hesitated, then looked Cady right in the eye. "Our friendship is important to me Cady, I truly value it. I hope you know that." He continued without giving Cady time to answer, "But there are things more important in life than friendship. I want you to know that I value your eternal life more than I value your friendship. I am willing to risk losing it for a chance to facilitate your salvation. I apologize for the way

I handled the conversation yesterday if I came across as sounding superior or having all the answers."

Cady felt humbled and off balance. "No harm done, no apology necessary."

"Did you speak about this with Shawna?" John asked.

"Yes," Cady admitted, feeling he had betrayed a confidence.

"And what did she say?"

"Well, she said to hear you out, just before I got mad and turned on the tube." Cady answered.

"And will you?" John asked.

"Will I what?"

"Will you hear me out?"

Cady wanted to scream, but instead nodded, not trusting himself to continue this ridiculous conversation.

"Tonight then?" John pressed. "Will you come over this evening and enjoy coffee and dessert with us while you listen?"

"Whoa, what's the hurry?" Cady moaned. "You're gettin' pushy here."

"Doug Peterson died last night, shot and killed on the job. Did you know him?" John asked, changing the subject. "Worked over at the 29th. I partnered with him when he was a rookie."

"No, hadn't heard. They get the guy?" Cady asked thinking as a cop would.

"Don't know," John said. "That's not my point. My point is he was either saved or not. Today he is in heaven for all eternity and will see his wife and family again or he would have remained forever in hell's torment. Jesus died so that we would live eternally with him in joy and happiness. But that choice has to be made before we die. There is no second chance."

Cady had nothing more to say; his brain was overwhelmed with what he had just heard. It echoed what he had heard as a child but had not understood. He knew now why it had been important to his mother and father and why they had been baptized those many years ago in anticipation of life after death.

John continued, "He and I partnered together for five years before we were comfortable enough to discuss religion, and he open up enough to ask questions about Jesus. He accepted Jesus and now walks with his Savior." John paused letting it all sink in. "Since no one knows how many days they have, I was not willing to wait five years before speaking to you about the good news of salvation."

Cady relaxed, tried to smile and said, "Tonight then, about seven o'clock?"

John nodded and smiled. "Seven o'clock will be fine. Please bring the girls also if you like."

~

When Cady called Shawna she seemed pleased and said she was looking forward to spending an evening with friends away from home. Cady was surprised when all three girls indicated they wanted to go along with them. The Days lived in a house just outside the city proper, which they had inherited from Helen's mother. The real estate was far more valuable than the house itself, being small and over 100 years old. But it actually had a yard, unlike the row houses all around it, that allowed them to have a dog and some privacy.

As they visited, before getting into the meat of the conversation, Cady was surprised to learn they were also transplants from the western states. Although they had been on the East Coast twenty plus years, their hearts still loved the open spaces of Colorado where they had met and married. Faith, Hope and Charity sat quietly listening to the conversation having been forewarned they could listen but not interrupt.

After they shared homemade cherry pie with a scoop of ice cream and coffee, John seated them in the small but comfortable living room then began to speak. "What I am going to share with you is the whole truth as I know and believe it, although I do not pretend to know all the answers to all the questions." He continued speaking, "As Cady knows, I am a man who likes things simple and uncomplicated, therefore my view of things is often that way also."

Everyone nodded, especially the girls relating to their new lives.

"I view the Holy Bible as God's truth without mistake or error as though it came from His very lips. It doesn't bother me that some argue against its accuracy, I choose to believe in it as it is written and interpreted. While some argue that men interpreted it and therefore diluted it, I believe that God worked within these men to keep His Word pure and true." Helen offered more coffee and soft drinks as John continued, "Can you agree with me on this point?" John stopped talking looking each in the eye while allowing them to consider his question to them.

"Yes," Shawna said, "I have no doubts about either God or His Word." She looked at Cady and then her children. "Girls, have you ever thought about this?"

Surprisingly, Cady heard his daughters talk about their experiences in Idaho at their small church where they had learned far more than he would have thought. They had attended AWANA on Monday evenings where they learned and memorized Scripture. Teachers there had helped them try to understand both the depth and the meaning of it. Cady wondered for a moment where he had been all those years while his family was growing up spiritually. Working, he guessed, pulling evening duty while Shawna took them to the church. All of a sudden he had the desire to make up for lost time, to bring himself up to speed where he could be in spiritual sync with his family.

"Yes," Cady said, nodding his head, "please continue."

John was visibly encouraged. "Okay then God is real, God is our creator, God's Word is inerrant. God created man in His image and likeness, without sin. But the first man and his wife sinned, setting themselves and all future generations apart from God, who cannot abide the presence of sin."

Helen quickly added, "God is perfect. Man became imperfect through sin. God wants community with us for all eternity, but that could never happen because man continues to sin. We could never have the relationship that Adam and Eve began with God because we were separated by sin."

The three Miller children jumped right in adding their wisdom to the conversation from memory. Cady again was shocked that he was the dim bulb in the group. Shawna also was well into her walk with Jesus and had a good understanding of the Bible message of salvation. Cady must have looked ill at ease or confused because when they spoke they looked directly at him.

First John said, "You see, God has provided a way for us to return to Him, for the sin in all of us to be forgiven so we may someday be fit to be with Him."

Then Helen said, "He sent His Son, Jesus, to earth with the intent that He would die so that we would never have to. Then He brought

Jesus back to life as He will also bring us back to life after we die the first death."

Cady's head was spinning as doors were slamming open and closed in his mind. It was as though he was no longer in control of his conscious thought process. His mind was going places and dragging him with it.

With the girls chirping in the background, Shawna laid the final brick, "And if you repent, say you are sorry that means, and really mean it, and ask Jesus to come into your heart, He will and you'll be saved." They each looked at each other for affirmation that they had not missed anything.

John added, "He'll begin to change you and although you will still sin, you will sin less and want to do better just to please Him."

Cady felt odd, kind of "short of breath" as though he had not been breathing for a few seconds, then kind of emotional, and overwrought. His heart raced. A quick thought flew into his mind, *Am I having a heart attack?* Just as quickly another replaced it, Y*es, ... an attack of the heart.* His heart was softening, opening like the petals of a flower embracing the morning dew, allowing Jesus to enter in. So he said the words, irrelevant of those around him, simply, "Forgive me, Jesus come."

The room was quiet with silent tears running down a dozen cheeks all at once. Seconds seemed like minutes as they basked in the "presence of the Lord."

Then John said, "Thank you Lord Jesus for our brother Cady Miller."

The girls squealed, Shawna beamed, and the Days smiled.

"Pie's gone, but I have homemade oatmeal cookies. Anyone for cookies and ice cream to celebrate?" Helen asked.

It was eleven o'clock on a school night before they arrived at home, and all were tired but excited. Cady had an early shift and the girls had homework, but no one seemed to care as their minds continued to work into the night. Interestingly, all were sitting down for breakfast at six o'clock still smiling and ready for the day.

Three

It began with them going with John and Helen to church then going even when John and Helen could not. The three girls were engaged in youth group and made friendships that carried them through the week at school. Shawna joined a women's Bible study and volunteered in the nursery during church. Eventually Cady was asked to serve as a deacon, making Christian friends who worked to maintain the church. When the widow came to the pastor asking guidance in selling her home, he gave her the Millers' name with his recommendation. So here they are, years later, living in her old house and rushing to John's bedside after his heart attack.

Smitty confirmed his original diagnosis, two arteries partially clogged, one forty percent and the other sixty percent. "He probably would not have even noticed had it not been for the wound and stress of the job. Two stints should make him feel better than he has in a long while. We'll give him time to recover and do a stress EKG and make sure we've missed nothing."

Although their travel plans were put on hold until spring, both John and Helen were grateful for the timing of the event. They applied for and received an additional work-related disability stipend added to their retirement, making their economic future more comfortable. Cady and Shawna allowed them to park the RV at their home where it served as a "get away" whenever they wanted to visit overnight.

At work Cady had a new partner, a rookie they nicknamed "Red" after his unruly mane of thick, red hair. He fit right in with everyone's image of an Irish cop: hard drinking, fighting, cussing, crude, tough guy.

They were so different that at first Cady had wanted to ask for a new partner. Red would come in late, hung over, telling tales, and bragging of his conquests. Cady had reminded himself that Red was twenty-six and single with no family or close friends. The commander had paired them well – the brashness of youth quieted by the hand of experience and age.

They had been together only two weeks when during a routine stop on the first day of August they were fired upon from a rented van. They had lost the van in heavy traffic and when it surfaced again a day later abandoned, sniffer dogs had indicated trace amounts of explosives in the cargo compartment. The matter had gone upstairs where it was shipped off to the feds, never to be heard of again.

They worked out together at the gym twice a week before their shift started. Cady wanted to maintain his strength and agility as his body slowed and aged. Red wanted to show off his strength and shirtless physique to other officers. Red kept pushing Cady to get into the ring with him, feeling the urge to prove himself to the veteran officer. Cady thought the "dance" was much like the ones he'd witnessed in Idaho where the young bull would try out the old bull for control of the herd. Like cattle, elk or deer the young feel the need to prove themselves. Finally it got to the point where other officers began to chide Cady for ducking the offer of his junior partner.

When word came down that they were going to pair off in the ring with gloves, it seemed the whole precinct showed up. Cady decided the victory had to be quick and decisive without humiliation if it were to benefit anyone at all. Experience had taught him that men could be friends after a fight if they were not forced to loose dignity, regardless of the outcome. The precinct chaplain was called in as referee. He quickly went over the few rules of engagement: gloves, no bare knuckles, no head butting, no hitting or kicking after a man was down, one round, last man standing won.

Cady stretched and warmed up before entering the ring wearing a T-shirt and trunks. Red waited for him, his nearly naked body rippled with muscle. They were about even in height with Red about 190 to 195 pounds. Without weighing Cady knew he'd never see 200 again but still looked fit at six feet three inches.

The two men circled, feigning punches and feeling one another out. Red threw a left that Cady gloved off moving counter clockwise before landing a hard right to Red's ribs. Cady, a southpaw, had not identified his style. He was jolted by a right that glanced off his glove into the side of his head. Cady tried to look dazed and wounded, stepping backward, hoping to lure Red toward him. Red's pride and eagerness to please the crowd was his undoing. As he moved forward, Red was already planning his next punch, not expecting Cady to sidestep him as he delivered a left jab to the jaw. The move both unnerved and upset the younger man. Finding himself sitting on his rump with his pride wounded, he jumped to his feet without thought, meeting Cady's powerful left with his chin. Cady stepped away and let him fall, eyes glazed, out on his feet.

The chaplain called it, raising Cady's hand before stooping to revive Red with the salts. As the young man's eyes opened he saw was his partner's ungloved hand reaching down to him to help him up.

"C'mon partner let's go have a shower then I'll buy us a beer," Cady offered.

After work they had a beer together. Cady then called Shawna to make sure she could feed a guest. Red shared dinner with the family and immediately the girls fell in love with "Uncle Red," the tall, handsome, funny-talking Irish guy.

It turned out that Red had just returned from doing three years with the Army in Afghanistan. He had dropped out of college in the second year, lacking finances to continue. Red, who was estranged from his family for unknown reasons, clearly enjoyed the closeness of the family unit and mentioned how much he missed his sisters.

At dinner the whole family made Red an offer he couldn't refuse, "Come to church with us, then come home and take a ride on one of our horses."

Red told them he was from a small farm in the South and hadn't ridden a horse since leaving home after high school. He agreed to their offer but started having second thoughts as the six of them approached the church. Clearly uncomfortable in the unfamiliar surroundings, Red sat back with the girls asking questions like a big brother would. Shawna, Cady, John and Helen in front of them.

After the service John asked Cady about work and what progress was being made on the investigation of the shooting that had nearly killed them both. To his surprise Cady had heard nothing and had all but forgotten it. He promised his friend to look into it then report back what he found out. He did mention the shooting and abandoned van, remembering then the similarity of the suspected cargo.

John raised his eyebrows questioningly, "Something going on we should know about?"

"Darn right," Cady returned. "Whatever it is we should know about it."

~

On the job the dynamics had changed. Red was listening more than he spoke, and he was eager to learn from his partner.

August 6 was hot and muggy as they cruised their beat. They had their windows up to keep out street sounds and heat.

The FBI had not returned Cady's calls, while his only contact in the CIA had nothing new to offer regarding the boat. He was surprised to find that none had heard about the van or its cargo from NYPD. His FBI friend promised to send a team over to Impound and go over the van for evidence and get back to him. The NYPD detectives working the shooting on the dock had come back empty-handed except for a match on one of the bullets from ballistics. An airport cargo employee at Newark International had been found shot to death, his body dumped with no identification. Again, sets of fingerprints matched, but were not on file anywhere in the database.

As Red neared an intersection, a taxi pulled from the curb violently causing him to brake hard to avoid a collision. Cady flipped on the lights and called it in with the intention of improving the cabbie's manners. The cabbie hit the boogie button and the chase was on.

What was it with people lately? A hundred dollar ticket or lose your license and your livelihood, plus a big fine. To Cady it seemed an easy choice.

A second car joined the chase when it became apparent there was more involved than a ticket as the taxi ran up on the sidewalk and began blowing through red lights.

Cady could clearly see the driver and three fares, all male with dark hair but little else, until they pulled up beside them at a light. Cady had his Glock in his hand when the passengers in the taxi opened fire on the squad car with automatic weapons. They missed both of Red and Cady but sprayed them with glass and disabled their radio. Cady holstered the Glock and grabbed the 12-gauge from its mount and fired through the broken window into the backseat of the taxi. The taxi lurched forward into the crowded intersection where it was hit and spun around. After it finally stalled the driver and front seat passenger fled on foot.

Cady was out of the vehicle in a second and used his hand unit to notify the station of the foot pursuit in progress.

Red exited on the far side and moved up beside him. "Where'd they go?" he asked.

Cady pointed at the side street that led to the warehouse district. "Down there. Check out the two in the backseat before you follow me. If they're alive, they are dangerous. Also we need air support so we don't lose them," he added over his shoulder.

A second squad car finally made its way through traffic and pulled in. Red brought them up to speed then headed for the taxi. As he reached for the door handle he took three in the vest through the closed door, knocking him to the pavement. Down, but unhurt, he fought to regain his breath.

The officers from the other car had skirted around to the far side before approaching the vehicle. A blast flattened them both and destroyed the taxi with its occupants. Red remained motionless for several seconds before gaining his feet and calling the station for help. Both officers were prone, bleeding from their ears, unconscious, but breathing.

A world gone mad, were the first thoughts that came to Red's mind. *Nothing is as it was, nothing will ever be the same again.* He thought about Pastor Orville's sermon in Revelation last week. *Could this be what he was describing?* Red made a mental note to return again to hear more about what the Bible had to say.

Cady called in on the radio. "Red, Red are you all right?"

"Yeah, I'm okay. Took three in the vest before they blew themselves up. If I'd not already been on the ground, I'd have been toast. I need to stay here with our other guys. The blast took them out."

"Bad?" was Cady's question.

"Bad, yeah but not fatal. They're both hurt but breathing."

"10-4," came the quick reply. "Did you get a chopper en route?"

"That's affirmative, you should have comm with it anytime," Red replied.

"Thanks, Cady out."

To Red's surprise the EMTs arrived on foot in ten minutes. The fire station was only two blocks away but with the traffic snarl, closer to an hour by vehicle. They took the vitals and seemed to like the results: BP good, heart rhythm strong and steady, eye reaction normal. Yet both remained unconscious for the first fifteen minutes after the explosion. The EMTs hooked up an IV with saline while continuing to monitor vitals. Red listened but did not understand the continuous medical dialogue going on between them and the station.

Other firemen arrived, also on foot. They attached a fifty-foot hand line to an adjacent fireplug to put out the burning taxi. Red could hear the rotors of a helicopter overhead. He hoped it may be police or medical rather than the "newsies," who took pride in informing everyone of everything, emphasizing their "right to know" above all things. The downed officers were relocated from the street to the roadside while waiting for the arrival of hospital transport. Red was grateful that the firemen, after extinguishing the fire, assumed traffic control duties to get traffic moving again. Already officers had begun rerouting traffic from the four incoming arterials away from the intersection. Red could hear "chatter" occasionally, from either Cady or others working with him in the pursuit of the fleeing suspects, but had no clear picture of what was going on.

Red heard the rotor noise and now the "wash" from the black chopper that was just above him. No markings identified it as police, civilian, or air ambulance. As it landed Red quickly deduced government. A team of men in excess of a dozen secured the area by pushing back the line of rubberneckers to the sidewalk before establishing a perimeter with crime scene tape. A team of four CSIs from Langley concentrated on the vehicle. They took samples and pictures, and bagging evidence, ignoring Red completely. Finally an ambulance arrived, taking away his two fallen comrades.

Red fingered two shell casings in his pocket. He had carefully picked them up from the pavement near the burning vehicle after the explosion, placed them in a gum wrapper and then in his pocket. Ordinarily he would have left them for the detectives and evidence squad, but he feared they would be lost or destroyed by the sea of onlookers.

Finally one of the "men in black" came over to him and spoke in a conciliatory tone. "Sorry about that. We needed to secure the scene and grab the evidence. I'm Johnson with the FBI. Can you tell me what happened here?"

Red nodded, nearly laughing at the statement before he began to speak. "I'm with the 23rd. We were pursuing a taxi with three passengers for entering traffic in an unsafe manner. It felt routine until they took flight in heavy traffic. We called it in and as we finally got in a position parallel to them they opened fire with automatic weapons. My partner returned fire with the 12-gauge that halted their progress and precipitated the accident. Two fled on foot, south toward the waterfront with him in pursuit. The two in the backseat hit me in the vest as I approached the vehicle before pulling the plug on themselves and injuring my backup."

"What can you tell me about the driver or passengers?" the FBI man asked. "Did you see their faces?"

Red thought a moment, recounting the events in his mind, before answering. "I had more of an impression than a visual. I was driving. Officer Miller, my partner, was closer and may have better descriptions. They and the driver were dark skinned, Latino or maybe Middle Eastern, dark hair, younger, clean shaven. Maybe it's just my prejudice showing, knowing that we have 10,000 taxi drivers from Pakistan and India driving the streets. Like I said, an impression rather than visual ident."

"Thanks. Not much left to see here. The forensics team will have to do the idents with dental and genetics." He handed Red his card. "Would you have your partner give me a call?"

Red nodded and pocketed the card before trying to contact Cady.

Red called in for instruction but mostly for an update on Cady's progress. He was told only that Cady and a team had followed the perps to the warehouse district near the waterfront but had no "eyes on them."

He was then told to return to the station. At the station his vehicle was taken to the motor pool for repairs.

As he entered the house the shift commander motioned him into his office and closed the door. "Tell me what you know," the commander said.

Red recounted the events in much the same way as he had to the FBI investigator. He then pulled the gum wrapper and its contents from his pocket laying it carefully on the desk before him.

The commander gave the rookie a stern look before speaking, "What are these? Am I to understand that you removed evidence from the scene?"

Red felt his face redden as he replied, "I did sir."

The commander settled back in his seat, "And you did knowing that evidence was to be collected by the CSI squad?"

Again Red nodded. "Yes, sir."

"Rookie, would you care to explain your actions in more detail to me?"

"Yes, sir. My motive was to preserve evidence that I felt was sure to be lost under the prevailing conditions with the crowd out of control and no way to secure the scene by myself. And," he continued after a short pause, "to make sure the evidence was followed up on by our own."

The commander was losing in his attempt to look stern and fearsome. "So you felt that breaking protocol would keep the chickens in our coop and not get lost down at the federal building?"

"Sir, the FBI had not arrived nor anyone else when I made the decision. There were a dozen shell casings on the ground, we had two men down, and citizens milling about the scene," Red spoke honestly. "I just secured a couple in case the rest disappeared as souvenirs."

The commander was smiling as he said, "And who besides you and I know you have them?"

"No one sir," Red replied. "I saw no reason to volunteer and no one asked. The FBI's team was already busy collecting their own."

"Quick thinking, Son," was the commander's reply. "Turn them over to Detective Sampson who'll have the lead in investigating the attack against you and Officer Miller."

"Sir, may I say one more thing?" the rookie asked.

Commander Davis nodded. "Go ahead."

"Thank you Commander. As you know, Officer Miller and his partner John Day were involved in a similar incident over a month ago. There has been no progress to our knowledge from any agency including our own. No one seems to be taking the lead or coordinating the investigation. It seems to have become a turf war between agencies jealous that someone else might one up them."

"That's out of line Rookie," said the commander. "I don't want to hear that kind of talk outside of this room."

Red nodded.

"However, inside this room say your piece," he said smiling broadly.

"I was going to make the suggestion that maybe this should go first to the team investigating the waterfront shooting to see if they tie together before opening up a separate investigation."

"You are a rookie, right? Only five months out of school, less than a month in the field?"

Red knew he had overstepped himself. "Yes, sir. I meant no disrespect. It's just that sometimes it seems like things get so involved and out of control that we overlook the obvious."

The commander spoke as though to himself. "My grandmother called it not being able to see the forest for the trees. Son, what do you see here?"

"Sir, something more than isolated events. It's way above my pay grade, but I agree with Miller and Day, something is going on here more than meets the eye."

"You've got good instincts, Rookie, as do both Officers Miller and Day. Both would have made good detectives but declined our offers. I'll personally deliver these to Detectives Noble and Barnes for follow up and look for a connection."

Red almost laughed as he had when he had heard that the two detectives had been purposely paired together. Tom Barnes and Burt Noble had forty combined years on the force, but only one together in the 23rd. The squad called them "the bookends," further making sport of their names.

"Thank you sir," Red said appreciatively. "Have you heard any word back about Miller?"

"No, last I heard we had two squads down there working with the 26th going from warehouse to warehouse with eyes overhead," the commander responded with concern in his voice. "Go ahead and write your report of the incident. I'll update you if I hear anything."

"Yes, sir, thank you sir," Red said before leaving.

~

Shawna's music station was interrupted by a breaking news bulletin causing her to turn on the television. News crews in helicopters were recounting the earlier events for the millionth time, rebroadcasting scenes of the intersection and explosion while they circled above the warehouses near the piers. As they brought the public up to date on the events they offered considerable speculation of their own as though they'd been eyewitnesses. Worry creased her bronze skin causing tiny wrinkles around her dark, almond eyes and at the corners of her mouth. She knew that these streets were the responsibility of the 23rd Precinct and that somehow Cady must be involved. They spoke now of two officers injured, multiple shots fired, and continuing pursuit. Against her better judgment she dialed the desk at the 23rd.

The desk sergeant answered the phone, "New York Police, 23rd Precinct. How may we help you?"

"Sorry Bill, this is Shawna Miller. Just heard the news. Are Cady and Red alright?"

"No specifics, but yes, they are fine. I'm told Cady is leading a pursuit of the two suspects who fired on them then fled."

"Thanks Bill," Shawna said. "Sorry to bother you."

He responded, "No bother. If I hear anything, will you be at home this afternoon?"

"I'll make a point of it," she answered before hanging up.

The summer sky was a mess, filled with television choppers that had to be constantly warned to keep their distance by the two NYPD surveillance ones that kept ground forces apprised of the progress. A perimeter had been set up on the ground while the eyes overhead looked for signs of attempts to flee. The warehouses were large – some filled with merchandise others empty and vacant. Cady led a squad of six men, being the only witness who could identify the perps. He interviewed dockworkers and warehouse men, and he also worked with two other squads when they encountered possible suspects. It was slow work. In three hours they had only eliminated four buildings, rousting their occupants and locking the buildings behind them.

As they entered S&S Imports, Cady was greeted by a small graying man with nervous eyes, seated behind a desk near the entrance.

"Anyone come or go in the last three hours?" Cady asked.

"No," came the reply.

"How many men are working in the warehouse now?" Cady asked.

"Just me," the nervous, little man said. "All the others left at four o'clock."

Something did not feel right to Cady. He turned to his squad and quietly voiced his concerns to be vigilant and wait for his signal. "Why didn't you leave with them?" Cady asked, trying to sound nonchalant.

When the man hesitated before answering Cady knew it was because he was fishing for an answer.

"Oh, just waiting for my ride," the man finally answered.

Cady noticed that the sign on the door still showed open for business. "Why don't you just wait outside with one of my officers then while we do a routine search."

One of the men escorted him out where he could be watched and out of harm's way.

The remaining five were quickly briefed as to Cady's suspicions and reminded that the two had automatic weapons and would kill without remorse.

"Remember," he said, "that man told us no one was in here. Move quietly and listen for movement. Everyone vested?"

They nodded affirmative before they paired up and moved slowly out away from the wall. The large open room was the length of a football field and half as wide. Most of the contents were on skids or pallets with little uniformity of size or height. The cargo doors appeared closed and locked from the inside.

Cady made contact with his eyes overhead. "We have a possible, not supposed to have anyone inside except blue. Keep an eye on all exits for us, please."

Moving slowly ahead they stopped often to listen and used hand signals. Cady knew if the suspects were inside and held their position they may never be seen. There was no way they could inspect and open all the containers and boxes large enough to hide a man.

Cady decided to play a hunch and advised the men of his intentions. Taking the bullhorn he yelled, "Allahu akbar!" He followed it up with three rounds in the air from the 12-gauge.

Within seconds they were under fire, his own words being repeated back to him. As automatic fire sprayed around them, they took refuge while watching for muzzle blasts that indicated their hiding place. When the noise subsided one of his men indicated he had seen movement on the top of a shipping container that had been stacked two high about a hundred feet ahead. While the suspects had the high ground and advantage of sight, they were also trapped with no way down. Cady called to command asking for backup to secure all outside entrances and for a sniper rifle, then settled in to wait.

It was obvious to him now that the men in the taxi were on some kind mission involving a radical Middle Eastern group. *Maybe it was bin Laden in the building with him who had been unable to resist the urge to answer his "Allahu Akbar" challenge, he thought as he waited.* Cady was not even sure what he had yelled, having read it somewhere or heard it on the news. The door opened behind them, an officer carrying an AR-15 with two clips made his way gingerly forward to Cady. Cady laid aside the bullhorn and the 12-gauge before finding a position behind a wooden crate about five feet in height. Quietly he jacked a round into the chamber, removed the lens caps from the scope, and swung down the bi-pod legs into position.

At full height both his head and much of his shoulders were visible above the crate, but in a shooters crouch only the rifle and his head could be targeted. The scope adjustment brought the container clearly into focus as he increased the power to seven. At this range he could see the whiskers on a mouse if there were one. Cady motioned two men to start flanking the container with the intention of causing the fugitives to move.

Once again they came under fire, bullets ricocheting off the cement floor. Cady cautioned the squad to be aware of poorly placed rounds that could glance and take out a leg or knee. He noted movement on the container and waited for his chance to return fire. It occurred to him that they had no fear of death and so chose to offer only their heads as targets. He hoped the possibility existed to disable and capture the suspects for interrogation but saw little chance. When his men moved again, the perps raised up to fire and Cady was ready to respond. A single shot from his AR-15 was rewarded by a gun falling from a lifeless hand above the container. The second man was up and running the length of the forty-five-foot shipping container when Cady pressed the trigger with the crosshairs on his left hip.

As they moved forward toward the container Cady hoped the shot was non-lethal but disabling. Cady advised air support of the situation and for his man outside to cuff the warehouseman. Cady was first to the ladder. He handed the AR-15 off and unholstered his Glock before beginning the climb up. He could hear movement but little else as he climbed. Cautiously he peered quickly above the top of the metal container then withdrew. One man was lifeless and was within just feet of the ladder. Another was some fifteen feet away trying to crawl toward a weapon lying at the edge of the container ten feet beyond him. In a single movement Cady rose above the container and shot three rounds at the weapon, sending it over the side and down to the cement below.

His enemy turned toward him, eyes filled with hate and a knife in his hand. He attempted to rise but was unable to gain his feet. Cady, having dealt with similar situations in military service, knew the man would kill himself rather than surrender. He dropped to one knee, took aim, and put two into the hand holding the knife. A scream of rage was the result as the knife dropped away. Cady called for help from the ground to secure the suspect and from outside for medical attention.

Cady was forced to pin the man down to prevent his attempted suicide by rolling off the container. He was cuffed hand and foot when the EMTs arrived. They secured him to a packboard and lowered him to the floor. The rifle round had taken out his hip joint and he was bleeding badly, and the Glock had made a mess of his hand.

Outside, the FBI had landed and taken command of the scene before sending men inside. Cady took a clean sheet from his ticket book, pressed it against the fingertips of the suspect's good hand, before folding it and putting it away. As Cady and his crew exited the building into the sunlight, he noted that everyone seemed to have a uniform that plainly advertised for their employer: CSI, NYPD, FBI. Cady called the precinct giving them a quick update before asking that someone call Shawna and set her mind at rest.

Shawna was relieved but still concerned when she took the call. She knew that debriefing would take a couple of hours and that Cady would be home very late. She put his dinner in the fridge before joining the girls on the couch in front of the TV. She reasoned correctly that they had seen the news bulletins also and worried for their father. She set their fears at rest before leading them in a prayer of thankfulness for God's protection.

At the station Cady took slaps on the back, ribbing, and affectionate criticisms from his fellow officers.

"Took him three shots to take the guy down."

"Hit him in the butt and hand."

"Cady needs some time on the range."

The watch commander called Cady in for the unofficial report much the same as he had Red. Cady walked him through the first part, nearly duplicating Red's recount, before going through the details of the pursuit and eventual capture of the suspect. After the boss stopped asking questions Cady leaned forward and carefully laid the folded ticket on the desk saying but one word, "Fingerprints."

The commander nearly laughed before saying, "You and your new rookie partner think our detectives need your help, obviously." He then placed the two shell casings beside the paper. "Please deliver both of these to the bookends for follow up, but keep it to yourself."

Cady walked in the door a little after eleven tired and hungry and found Shawna still up waiting for him. She gave him a kiss then put the meatloaf and scalloped potatoes in the microwave before handing him a tall cold glass of milk. He went right to the girls' rooms where he spent a few minutes thanking God for them and kissing their foreheads. He then returned to the kitchen. Eating slowly and talking between bites, he walked through the events of the day, downplaying the exchanges of weapon fire. At midnight, having showered, he crawled into bed beside Shawna and went right off to sleep in her arms.

~

God is gracious. Cady was not scheduled to work the following day, allowing the family to enjoy breakfast together. Before promising to rent a movie to watch with bushels of popcorn, he hugged each explaining to them how fathers felt about daughters for the hundredth time. When the girls went outside to feed and ride the horses, Cady swept Shawna into his arms and told her how husbands felt about their wives.

It was mid-afternoon when the phone rang. It was Barnes with a report on the fingerprints. Those he had taken from the captured man ended up matching the one on the shell casings from the boat and the airport murder. Those from the two who had shot Red came back with no match. Additionally there had been both weapons and explosives in the warehouse. Cady thanked him for the report then called John at home. Cady could tell John itched to get back on the horse, knowing also that he never could. He then called his contact at the FBI hoping to exchange information but finding him unresponsive or without information to share. He called the number on the card that Red had given him only to be chastened for not sharing the information earlier. *Turf wars*, he thought to himself, *afraid cooperation will give someone else the chance to make the basket rather than themselves. They needed a good coach to remind them this was a team sport.*

After he called Red at home and shared what little he had learned he called Johnson back setting an appointment to meet with him. Cady intentionally misled him by promising additional information in an attempt to get an interview with the prisoner. Brushing the dust off, Cady began to reread some of the psych manuals left from his short training with the FBI. In particular he wanted information to guide him in the nuances of interrogation among the Islamic community. As he had when yelling "Allahu akbar" in the warehouse, he hoped to use their fanaticism against them. It was well known that most would rather die than betray their faith, but many might let information slip out in a moment of careless rage.

It appeared to Cady and most other law enforcement agencies that the feds marched to a different drummer often able to make up rules as they went along. When he arrived he was greeted with respect. Johnson most likely looked up Cady's file and had been surprised at his credentials.

They fenced for a few minutes before Cady came right out and asked, "Is the subject being held on the premises?

Johnson hesitated then nodded the affirmative. "Being held in solitary confinement without outside contact."

"Has interrogation given us anything conclusive to tie it to the other events?" Cady asked.

Johnson noted the skillful way Cady had included himself in the ranks of the FBI community with the simple word "us." *This street cop must have been a quick study in his short stay at Quantico*, he thought. "Nothing of value, I am afraid," Johnson answered. "He has admitted only that he is here on a jihad, which failed to bring the expected glory to Allah."

"Anything to tie him to known radicals?" Cady continued.

"I am afraid I am not permitted to share this information," Johnson answered with seeming sincerity.

"I expect not. Wouldn't do to work together and share the limelight," Cady countered, but not harshly.

Johnson shrugged but said nothing.

"Mr. Johnson, let me tell you why I am here," Cady said.

Johnson smiled. "I was wondering when you'd get around to that."

Cady continued while looking Johnson squarely in the eyes, "I was shot, one of my partners killed, the other badly wounded and forced to retire early, a baggage handler at the airport also killed, two officers from my precinct were wounded by the blast, and this guy's three buddies killed." Cady stopped for effect. "Something's going on, you know it and I know it, and yet you have no idea of what it is. Does that about cover it?"

Johnson smiled then asked, "What do you want from me today?"

Cady waited a moment then said, "An interview with the subject. Short and sweet, in and out. Let me interrogate him myself."

Johnson raised an eyebrow. "So you think you can succeed where our trained men have failed?"

Cady calmed himself. "Not necessarily, but possibly. What could it hurt? You'd be right there watching us through the glass. You've got squat now and sooner or later you'll have to give him access to legal."

Johnson seemed to consider the idea before saying, "I don't have authority."

"Who does?" Cady came back. "Let me talk to him."

"How would you handle it?" Johnson questioned. "Beat it out of him?"

"If I thought it would work, maybe. But we both know it wouldn't," answered Cady. "I hoped to come at him from a different angle, get him off balance, maybe get him to slip and open up before he knew it."

"You need a job?" Johnson asked smiling. "Seems you are a quick learner. Give me a few minutes while I see what I can do."

Cady sipped black coffee while he waited for Johnson to return. About a half-hour later Johnson entered with another man, a man Cady knew well.

Al stuck out his hand and smiled. "Miller, so nice of you to visit us again."

Cady had been in Al's unit, his CO in Iraq. He was also the one who had cleared the way for Cady to receive training at Quantico. Al had hoped to recruit Cady but had failed because of Cady's commitment to his family.

Still smiling, Al continued, "So you think your three-day training with us makes you the go-to man for further interrogation?"

Cady was not smiling. "It didn't hurt, but what I bring to the table is that I was there, looked him in the eyes, took away his dream of martyrdom, killed his friend – he hates me. Not the same way he hates all infidels, but personally. I think I might get under his skin enough to cause him to screw up."

Al and Johnson looked at each other, the genius of the plan was suddenly apparent to them.

"Done," answered Al. "When would you want to do it?"

Cady responded smiling, "No sense of driving all the way home just to come back. How about giving me a half-hour to organize my thoughts?"

"We'll bring him down then come and get you," Al said. "Good to see you again."

Exactly thirty minutes later Johnson opened the door. "He's ready. You need anything before we go in?"

"Do you still have a vending machine?" Cady asked.

"Sure," Al affirmed. "What can I getcha?"

"How about two sodas and a package of pork rinds," Cady answered

The room looked just like on TV: small, drab, with a metal table attached to the floor. The prisoner, handcuffed to the table ring, sat in a wheelchair facing the mirrored wall. Cady had stripped to his T-shirt and jeans and made sure the room temperature was set at eighty plus degrees. Johnson opened the door for him before retiring to the next room where he joined Al.

Cady began, "Hello again, remember me? How's the hand doing? I see you are not walking yet." The silent sullen look told Cady that he was well remembered. "Got some bad news for you – we found your stash of weapons and C-4. We gave it to the Israeli consulate. Oh, and your buddies said to tell you that Allah is a joke, they're in hell right now without a single virgin in sight."

Cady needled him, keeping his voice light and nonthreatening, "Here, you want a pig skin?" he said, holding the bag toward him.

Finally the man screamed something unflattering at Cady before spitting toward him. Cady continued to smile, popping the top of the soda open.

"You thirsty?" Cady took a long draw on the can, noting how good it tasted in the hot, stuffy room. Chewing the skins noisily and sucking down the drink, Cady continued, "So Amad, what you doin' in town? Just visiting or planning to stay and open a Mr. Pig franchise?"

Both hatred and sweat dripped from the veiled eyelids as the man continued to sit silently staring back at Cady.

"Did you hear about the one where we bombed Mecca with 100,000 smoked hams? We called the operation, 'Pigs in a Blanket.'"

Another insane scream followed with cursing and threats. "Infidel pig! I am not the only one. There are many more who are even now on your soil waiting for the signal to glorify Allah. Soon, very soon now you'll not be making such jokes with your wives and children lying dead in the streets. You think you are so smart. How will you stop us? You don't even know us. You continue to invite us to your shores expecting that we will become like you. But we will never be like you."

Cady and the FBI men were listening carefully, recording every word and gesture on film.

When he hesitated, Cady spoke again. "Sounds like a plan alright, but I already told you we have your stash. Whatcha gonna do, taxicab us to death? I can see it now 10,000 taxis with towel heads behind the wheel all screaming, 'Allahu akbar!' racing down Madison Avenue."

As he finished speaking he intentionally spilled the pig skins across the table into the prisoner's lap. The dark face went white, black eyes smoldered as he attempted to stand without success, unable to reach the offending morsels with his handcuffed hands.

He screamed, the sound bordering on fear, before he yelled, "When they fall, you will know that Allah is god!"

"Who are they, Amad?"

"The roofs of your little temples. He abruptly stopped speaking again.

Cady knew that he knew he had told too much. *But to what may he be referring? They? More than one. More than one what? National monuments, federal buildings, schools, hospitals, churches, what? And how? Obviously they had smuggled in explosives. Maybe there were more, but where? Was the target New York or the whole East Coast? How about the Capitol? Smart money knew that man's security was no security at all. Only God could protect completely.*

"Amad, I wonder if you will ever be able to face Mecca again what with all that pork in your lap and all. You already missed the witching hour for today. Is there a penalty for skipping a day? Do you lose your turban or something?"

The two behind the glass were cracking up, tears running down their cheeks.

"Well Amad, it has been fun visiting with you, but I've got to run, got to talk to two more of your buddies. We captured two who aren't quite so faithful as you, more willing to share information. No, don't get up, I'll see my way out," Cady said standing.

"Liar, none of the faithful would talk to you. We have sworn to die," spat the prisoner. "The symbols of your decadence will soon lie in ruin."

Cady popped another soda as he left the room, closing the door behind him. The conditioned air bathed his face as he sat down to visit with Al and Johnson.

"Quite an act I have to admit," Al said. "You ever think of stand up?"

Cady nursed his soda before answering," Did we get anything useful?"

Johnson replied, "Probably too soon to know. Need to have our guys go over it piece by piece. I did get that there is more than one target, that the targets were chosen to humiliate our country before the world, and that the event is imminent."

Al took up the analysis, "This is not a random event, probably involves many operatives at more than one location. It is unlikely that unless we catch a break we can prevent them all."

Cady nodded. "I agree. Probably well financed, sometime in the planning, and he was right when he said we cannot protect everything all the time. Does the CIA have any intel to factor into the case?"

Al replied, "A lot of whispers but nothing of substance. I'll arrange a meeting with the White House and ask them to invite all the players to cooperate. I think we have a viable threat to our nation's security. And thank you, Mr. Miller, you did indeed make my day."

Cady just smiled as he took his friend's hands, thanking them for the snacks.

On the long trip home he took a few moments to thank God for today's victories and ask Him for His protection in the future. Cady called home giving Shawna a guess as to his ETA but no information about the events of the day. A dark cloud began to gather in his mind, as it often did when he stepped away from God and depended upon his own resources. As he worked to see through the smoke and haze he became more and more uncertain and fearful. He prayed, "In your will, grant me the wisdom to see what others cannot see and do what others cannot do. Amen."

Four

Cady asked the commander to invite Red, Noble and Barnes into his office that he might share what little he had learned. He asked them not to leak the information to those who might put it on the street causing the enemy to go into deep cover. Having listened carefully, each had thoughts and ideas to share. The commander pledged to try and get a copy of the interview for them to dissect. Red suggested that Cady invent a couple of probable suspects on the FBI terrorist list then return and spend some time with the turbaned tornado. They all laughed at his humor before agreeing that the plan may hold merit. Cady agreed to make a call to Al and get his opinion. The two officers who had been hurt in the bomb blast were not seriously injured but remained on medical leave with hearing issues.

John, eager to be included in the ongoing drama, called Cady's home several times, missing him each time. Cady and Shawna drove over to their house for a visit, happy to find John looking robust and sassy. As the women talked, Helen indicated that the stint had worked well. Dr. Smitty had given him a clean bill of health. John was eager to praise God for the timing of the event that had likely prevented him from a more serious or fatal one.

Privately, Cady recounted the events of the interrogation as well as memory would permit, but lacking much of the humor that made it so effective. John promised to add his skills to the mix in an attempt to narrow down the list of potential targets. He also suggested that Cady spend some time with a Muslim-turned-Christian convert in their church and ask for his input.

~

In North Carolina, a state patrolman had made a routine traffic stop before detaining two foreign nationals from Jordan with borrowed driver's licenses. They claimed to have borrowed them from family members so they could rent a car while vacationing in Florida. A hasty computer check showed no wants or warrants on either the driver or his passenger. They were both released after posting bail and being instructed to return for trial.

~

Ben, Phyllis and their children had just returned from vacation in Cancun when he got a call from his uncle. Cady was hoping to catch them before school started for the fall to invite them up north for a visit. Unfortunately by the time they connected it was too late but Ben promised a visit the first three-day weekend they could schedule in, maybe Labor Day. Cady's three girls loved to mother Ben's younger children, always treating them like royal guests.

~

Behind the scenes the NYPD police commissioner, mayor, and law enforcement's upper echelon met behind closed doors with the FBI unit assigned to the ongoing investigation. Twenty-two possible targets were identified including the Statue of Liberty, the U.N. Building, as well as other notables in the Big Apple and surrounding area. Bomb-sniffing dogs and special explosives units were hastily making the rounds of hundreds of thousands of square feet of foundations, equipment rooms, utility tunnels, and basements trying to look unobtrusive and routine in their searches. Demolition experts accompanied them pointing out the most susceptible areas in each structure as they went.

In a seemingly unrelated incident, Florida state troopers had found the bodies of three men and a woman ran a training and certification school for fixed-wing aircraft from their own private airport. One of the charter planes was missing and later was found abandoned at Newark International. Florida investigators had it earmarked as a drug smuggling incident gone bad but had not yet made a connection.

~

With John in tow, Cady entered the 23rd going right to the commander's office. While John had no official standing as law enforcement he was warmly welcomed as he entered the squad room, and took a chiding for having taken early retirement. After exchanging pleasantries they were invited to sit and were asked the nature of their call since Cady was off duty. John spoke first, establishing his right to pursue his attackers as his credentials to be included in the investigation. He, like his former partner, was convinced that though they had interrupted a jihad in progress it had been but delayed. The watch commander was one of four lieutenants who operated under the captain of the precinct. The captain answered to one of the several chiefs in each borough, and the chiefs were under the command of the commissioner. In short he at most had the ear of his captain who might make a case to his chief. They had the wrong audience to accomplish anything, but did get his endorsement to make their case directly to the captain.

They both knew this in advance but knew also there was a protocol to follow before they went over their lieutenant's head. John, having worked in several precincts, knew the chief personally at the 26th as he had been his captain years before. Cady knew that the 26th had been involved when they searched and found the perps in the warehouse. He hoped that they might use their combined influence to call a joint meeting of both captains and chiefs to listen to them. Unknown to him, this meeting had already taken place from the top down. Sadly little information from the top made it to the streets and little from the streets caught the interest of those at the top.

Thursday morning at nine o'clock they were welcomed into Chief Jordan's office where their own chief and both captains were already seated. Cady felt a little intimidated when they entered but was encouraged when John went right over to the chief and shook hands like the old friends they were. His own captain and chief stood and acknowledged him as Officer Miller.

They were about a half-hour into their presentation when the chief arose and stopped them. "Officers, while you have added some dimension from the street perspective, which we appreciate, there is little that we have not just recently discussed at length with our superiors. Let us congratulate you both on having the vision to see and try to prevent further danger to our city."

Both captains who also had not been included in the top-level summit turned and looked at each other.

"So," Captain Fred Thompson said a bit too loudly, "there is a behind-the-scenes investigation going on, but we have not been privileged to be included?"

"Welcome to our world," John said softly, but audibly. "'Need to know' is what the commissioner and mayor called it. They were afraid that if the word got out on the street that number one the public might panic, and number two the organization may go underground until we let down our guard and then complete their mission."

Chief Jordan resumed speaking, "Sorry Fred, it was not our call – and this information cannot leave this room, are we clear on that?"

Cady replied, passion filling his voice, "So the time we have spent trying to get someone, anyone, looking seriously at this has not been wasted? The FBI boys have not just been blowing smoke up our butts?"

Jordan smiled. "Officer Miller, I am not sure that I can agree to a certainty of the FBI's commitment, but I can say we are, as we speak, utilizing over a hundred men daily to investigate probable targets."

When John resumed speaking, tensions had lessened. "I don't suppose you could include a couple of country boys in the need to know circle could you Chief?"

"Officially you know better than that, John. Unofficially I welcome either of you to call and invite me to lunch at any time. Who knows where our conversations might lead."

Both chiefs stood. Chief Jordan addressed the captains, "Men it goes without saying that you are now on the inside of the investigation. Carry the weight of that responsibility carefully."

~

On August 22, Cady and Red were on routine patrol together. They took a 10-16, a domestic, and made two traffic stops before the squawk came over the radio.

"Shots fired, shots fired, 43rd and 6th streets. Victim down. Two suspects fleeing south on foot."

They took the call while another unit arrived on the scene with an ambulance behind. Cady called in a 10-32, man with a gun, before driving south on 6th Street without lights or siren. He observed the pedestrian traffic until people began to point at the fleeing suspects down the block. Because of the potential danger for injury to bystanders or hostages, Cady turned left at the intersection so he wouldn't be seen. When he called for backup he briefly described the situation and recommended that backup remain out of sight at 45th and let the suspects come to them. He and Red parked and proceeded on foot through the adjacent alley toward 6th Street.

New Yorkers, Cady thought, *they'd stand there watching right in the way until they became victims.* He wondered if he'd ever understand the East Coast mentality.

Sometimes the blue brought respect, demanded attention, and gave the officer the edge. Other times like this just announced his presence giving the bad guys visual identification and a clear target. As they approached 6th they slowed, weapons drawn. Cady said a silent prayer for them all, asking for God's protection and direction.

The alley emptied out onto 6th at the midpoint between 44th and 45th. As he and Red cautiously stuck their heads around the corner they could see two young men with dark skinned rapidly approaching and pushing angry pedestrians aside. Cady hit his mic and gave an update to his backup and the station indicating that they would attempt to take them as they passed the alley. If they failed, the unit at 45th would provide the option.

As both men hugged the wall, Cady whispered to Red, "As soon as we have visual, I'll attempt to take them out with a body check, knocking them to the ground. You stand ready to use your weapon as necessary."

Red started to offer that he was younger and stronger and should make the physical contact but did not. Instead he just nodded. It was not the time to question the veteran's decisions. Before the two could register alarm as the alleyway opened up to them, Cady hit the inside man low and hard pushing him into the other. All three of them tumbled across the sidewalk toward the street. Red had his weapon trained on the pile shouting orders and threats meant to disarm them. The man under Cady attempted to struggle to his feet but was easily restrained by a strong forearm across his windpipe. The outside man had hit the pavement hard with his head and seemed bewildered as he got to his feet still holding his gun. Red ordered him twice to drop the weapon before taking aim at him. The man made no move to either raise the weapon or to drop it. He just stood looking down on Cady and his partner as though an observer. He was still standing, posing no immediate threat, when backup arrived from 45th Street. He was soon stripped of his weapon and pushed to the ground before being cuffed while Red continued to hold his weapon at the ready.

Cady had his man cuffed and was attempting to straighten his uniform as he walked toward his partner. "Nice job Red," he said sincerely. "Some would have been quick to shoot seeing it as the only option while taking a life and endangering the crowd around them."

Red found his voice and answered his mentor, "I thought about it and would have if he'd have raised his weapon. He looked kind of out of it, out on his feet. Kind of like I felt in the ring after you hit me."

They both laughed. Cady nodded. "We should probably mention that in our report in case he needs medical attention for a head injury."

Back in their unit Cady complained that he'd just totaled another fifty-dollar pair of uniform pants, pointing to the badly scuffed knee where the pavement had tried to wear through it.

Red laughed before responding, "Old man, when are you going to step back and let me rip up a pair and save you money to raise your family?"

There was both humor and truth to be found in the question.

Cady picked up on both then answered, "Next time Rookie, next time. You are right. You should have equal opportunity to get scuffed up. You've earned it."

They both laughed again. At the house they turned their report over to the detectives who'd been assigned the case and inquired about the shooting victim.

"Prelim from witnesses makes the victim the initiator of the event. He shot first and missed. They took him down then panicked and ran. They were carrying an unregistered but neither has a record. Just locals trying to protect themselves it looks like. They'll likely do time for possession of an unregistered weapon. That will probably ruin their lives. By the time they get out they'll be punks."

Cady nodded, concurring with the detective's appraisal of the situation. "If they'd not had a weapon they'd have died, but because they did their lives will never be the same. Man's rules, man's justice – always flawed. Laws were meant to protect men from themselves and are disregarded by those from whom you need protection the most. Are they here in the house?" Cady asked.

"One is upstairs. His brother is down at county having tests. They think you gave him a concussion. How long since you played football?" The three laughed.

Cady called home, as his shift ended, telling Shawna he'd like to take some time to check up on the two boys before leaving. He could see her nod over the phone, a smile crossing her lips, knowing he'd need to make sure he'd have caused no permanent injury.

As Red overheard the conversation he asked, "May I come with you?"

"Sure, let's go upstairs first then out to the hospital and see what we find."

~

Ted was taken from the holding cell into interrogation where Cady and Red joined him. It was obvious to Cady that he was a young African American, probably under twenty.

Why do we do that? Cady thought to himself. *We segregate people under the pretense of giving them an identity they never knew or earned. Why not American? Why does man have to associate a God given characteristic special meaning that causes others to set them apart?*

In the beginning Ted tried to act tough, giving smart answers, and using street talk to answer their questions. However, when Cady asked about his brother his demeanor changed and he became a small, frightened boy. The boys were brothers with Ted the oldest at seventeen and Tom only sixteen. They had lived with their mother all their lives in the very neighborhood where they were captured. Red was surprised to find that they were both still in school. Before leaving, Cady promised to check on Tom and let Ted know what he found out.

Red rode along unusually quiet on the way to County before making the statement, "I could have just as easily killed him."

Cady knew that Red was replaying the event in his mind, factoring in the new information they had just received. He didn't respond for a while then said, "God loves us all, the ones we call the bad ones and the ones we call the good ones. To Him we are all sinful, but we carry a piece of Him inside us giving us potential to be perfect. When I prayed in the alley I included them in my prayers also, knowing that God loved them too."

At County hospital the officers were directed to a room where security stood at the door. At first the nursing staff thought that they were there to take the patient into custody and transport him to jail. In the room Tom was handcuffed to the bed rail and his eyes were closed. His dark hair and skin contrasted with the whiteness of the dressing on his head. His eyes immediately opened when he heard their footsteps, and he had the look of a caged animal.

"Tom we have come from visiting with your brother, Ted," Cady said softly. "He asked that we check on you and let him know how you are doing."

Tom started to speak then shut his mouth without a word.

Cady continued, ""Do you need anything, water or something to eat?"

With smoldering black eyes, Tom tenuously looked Cady over while remaining silent.

"Has your mother been up yet?"

With the mention of his mother, Tom began to cry. Large tears silently streaked his mahogany cheeks.

They moved closer and Cady continued, "It'll be alright Son. God will help you through this. Do you believe in God?"

For the first time Tom's lips moved, with words too faint to hear.

"Do you know Jesus?" Cady continued.

"I messed up," came the reply. "We shoulda been in school. Ted tol' me so, but I wouldn't listen. I wanted to play the games. He jus' came 'long to keep me from gettin' in trouble. Didn't work tho, got in trouble 'nyway. Duke n' Griff been wantin' us to work fo' 'em, peddelin' the stuff in school. We tol' 'em no, but you cain't tell Griff 'no' so he start shootin' at us. I never shot a gun 'fore. Did I kill 'im?"

"No, Son, he's going to make it," Cady answered.

Tom started to cry again. "Now I really messed things up. I'm goin' to jail. He'll get out an' come after Mom or Ted an' I can't help 'em."

"You pray?" Red asked the boy, surprising Cady.

"Some," came the answer.

"How about we pray together now," Red continued. "Let God work out all the details and protect your mama."

Tom looked at him with tear-filled eyes then bowed his head and began moving his lips. Cady and Red prayed silently with him for salvation in Jesus, for change and direction in their lives, and for His perfect will for their future. They had just raised their heads when they became aware of another person in the room. A tall, thin black woman wearing the uniform of a maid had entered but waited until they had finished to speak.

"You the ones who brought in my boys?" she asked matter-of-factly.

"Yes, ma'am," Cady answered for them both. "We're not here officially as officers, just checking up on the boys. We talked to Ted before we came down."

"They're not bad boys you know," she said to no one in particular. "Time was when their daddy was alive we's all doing pretty good. Their daddy was in the Air Force, shot down and kill'd in Iraq. Jus' gettin' by since." She seemed to come back from where ever she'd been and looked Cady straight in the eye. "They goin' to jail?"

Cady thought before answering. "I can't say for sure. We don't make those decisions. It's up to the courts. Can say though we'll be prayin' for them. We'll give them all the help we can, speak up for them in court. But carrying a weapon is a serious charge."

She nodded her assent. "Sure is, I shoulda got rid 'o it. It was his daddy's. Come back with him an' his personal belongings from the war. I kept it with his medals for when the boys grow up and it mean somethin' to 'em."

They said goodbye then returned to the jail where they gave Ted the update on his brother before heading home. The drive was over an hour each way, each day. Many had asked Cady if he hated the commute, to which he always smiled and said, "Heck no, best part of my day is spent praying, looking at God's creation all around me, listening to the radio preachers, and preparing for my destination." Unknown to them he was not referring to his arrival at home or work.

Shawna and the girls had waited to eat with him making him feel a little guilty but a lot loved. It was not his practice to share the events of his day with the family, generally preferring to shelter them from its sordid details. But this day felt different. There seemed to be lessons to teach and to learn.

He related the story as he now knew it about the two boys, their father, mother, poor choices, and probable penalties for those choices. All three daughters participated in the discussion that followed, giving their opinions and asking questions. Shawna remained quiet, content to watch and listen to her little brood. Before sending them off to bed, the family prayed together and they included the brothers in their petitions.

When they were alone Shawna smiled and said, "So how much did you make today after you subtract the cost of the new pants?"

He countered, "Uniforms are a tax deduction."

She came right back, "If you keep this up we'll have nothing to deduct it from."

They went off to bed to share the closeness God had designed for them.

~

The CIA received through various sources credible intel of imminent threats against America. Not unusual at all in number because of the many embassies and military bases across the globe but unusual in that they seemed more aimed at American soil. FBI operatives received instruction to be more vigilant on incoming potential terrorists concentrating on the borders and incoming aircraft. Unknown to the American public, several had already been detained, questioned, jailed or deported as circumstance dictated. Our own form of government and the freedoms we so highly prize are also our weaknesses when considering the nation's security. Even America's enemies have rights in America. Many are ready to go to court to assure they are defended to the point of foolishness.

One of Cady's conundrums was trying to deal with why a known lawbreaker must be allowed to repeat his bad behavior before protecting the public from him. While he may have been prone to err on the side of the victim, the law protected the rights of the accused over the rights of the victims. Joyfully he had never desired to be a judge.

~

One evening late in August, as school was commencing, Ben called the Miller home and left a telephone message. "We will all be able to come up for a visit over Labor Day if that works for you. Mom may join us also if you have room. Get back to us when you can. Love you all,

Uncle Ben." Ben loved to consider himself Uncle Ben for the sake of the three Miller girls, as Cady had been Uncle Cady to him.

When the Millers returned from Bible study and heard the news they were jacked. Although it was late Cady was forced to call right back to Uncle Ben and confirm their eagerness to see them.

A call to John the next day confirmed that the RV was available as an extra bedroom for the overflow crowd they were expecting. While on the phone, John offered that he had spoken to his Iranian Christian friend at church the past Sunday and asked him to keep an ear to the ground concerning potential bombings. It had been a touchy situation with the man having mixed allegiances being still new to the faith.

Cady made a call to his FBI contact only to find him out of the office. He left a short and to the point message before heading into town for his shift. Red had already signed in and had been upstairs visiting with Ted before Cady came in. Arraignment for both boys was scheduled for Friday, two days away. Cady thanked Red and called the DA's office and found that Sarah Mitchell had the case but was currently in court. He left a message for her to return his call. Morning was routine with a fender bender, a billing dispute at a cafe, and a shouting match at a convenience store over a lotto ticket number. At coffee break Cady called Shawna at work, which he seldom did. When she answered he could hear fear in her voice. He began his conversation with, "Everything's fine. I just need your help on something."

He hoped to enlist her aid and that of her organization when trying to convince the DA and the court system that the boys would do better under supervision than incarcerated. He was hoping that the judge was willing to try rehabilitation for the youthful offenders.

With the donuts barely settled in their stomachs and the coffee waiting to be purged, Cady's cell phone rang. It was Sarah Mitchell. He had worked with her on several prior cases but had not been put on her witness list up to this point regarding Ted and Tom. Cady knew that court was in session and she was calling as a courtesy while on recess, so he asked her if they could meet in person as her time allowed. He knew he could better plead his case one-on-one rather than on the phone to a busy assistant district attorney.

"Nine a.m., my office, but I only have a few minutes. Is this about a case?" she asked.

"Yes, I'll see you there, and thanks," Cady said to the dial tone.

Afternoon was also routine until the desk sergeant let Cady know he had a personal to return from Chief Jordan at the 26th. Cady could hear the unanswered question in his voice as he delivered the message.

"Chief, this is Officer Miller returning your call."

"Yes, Miller, I'd hoped you'd be calling with a lunch invitation," he laughed. "I have a little bit of updated information for you concerning our last conversation."

"Sir, can we make it tomorrow, and may I invite John to join us?" Cady asked.

"Most certainly. John and I go back a long way. He has a good mind and remains an asset to the city of New York," the chief said.

They set a time and place with the chief volunteering to clear it with Cady's watch commander.

When morning came Cady checked it at the 23rd letting the commander know he had a nine o'clock with the DA concerning the shooting case but did not volunteer the details of the visit. Sarah, as always, was overworked and understaffed. Her success was not in her great abilities but in her work ethic. She never went to court unprepared, never. Her conviction rate showed it. She also was an idealist who really believed in the system and the law as the only differentiation between man and animals.

"What do you have to offer me Officer Miller that will bring justice to our great city," she asked tongue in cheek.

She was a strawberry blonde, early thirties, never married, trim and athletic, but plain as a paper bag until she smiled. She was smiling now. Even though she never flirted or messed around, she had flirty eyes and a girl-like disposition that made you want to smile too.

"Time's a wastin' Cady. What's on your mind?"

"Two young men, to most throw-aways, to me boys at a cross roads. I am speaking of course about the Brown boys, Ted and Tom, who were involved in a shooting last week."

"A slam dunk, Cady. You caught them red-handed with an unlicensed firearm in their possession. Forget that it was used in a questionable shooting just prior," she came back. "Do you want to testify? Is that it? Never saw you as a glory hound, but you could ice the cake for me."

"Yes, and no, Sarah," Cady answered. If you need me to testify after I tell you what I came for, I will. It's your call. I want you to consider giving them a chance to have a life, a life off the streets without criminal records. The life their father died in Iraq for."

She settled back in her seat. "I'm listening."

"Yes, we took them down, down hard. I gave the younger one, Ted, a concussion. I have a little background to offer over and above the obvious. Their father was a fighter pilot, shot down and killed protecting our freedom. The gun they used was his weapon shipped home with his body as part of his legacy. It was unlicensed because their mother never considered it as a weapon but as their inheritance when they were grown, just as are his uniform and medals. Their mother has raised them alone, working and living on his survivor's benefits without male influence to guide them as they became men. They have never been in trouble. Both carry good grades in public school. They don't do drugs and they don't have any discipline problems. They're under pressure from the local drug dealers to work for them. Tom made a bad call when he took the weapon with him for protection from them. Ted was along just to look out for his kid brother when he cut class to play arcade games. Both boys are trying hard to stay out of gangs, stay in school, and make their mother proud – tall order for a couple of black kids without a dad."

Sarah' s mind had been running ahead of the story when she asked, "So we just look the other way and give the public an okay to carry illegal guns if you have a good reason? What kind of a message does that send?"

Cady was ready. "Good point, Sarah. But what kind of a message does it send to those trying hard and find no one cares?"

Sarah looked at her watch. "I have a suspicion there's more, Officer Miller. What's on your mind?"

"Both are minors," Cady answered. "Put them on supervised probation until they are of age. Give them community service. If they stay clean expunge their records, and if they mess up come down on them hard."

"We don't have a budget for supervised parole for every kid who gets himself in trouble," Sarah countered.

"Is it cheaper to put them in juvie where they'll learn to become what we expect them to be, thugs? What if I told you that you could do it for free?" Cady asked.

"Officer Miller, don't you have enough on your plate already with a family of your own?" she asked looking hard at him.

"Yes, ma'am, I certainly do," Cady said smiling. "But I know a couple who do not, recently retired officer John Day and his wife, Helen. I might add that Shawna, my wife, works in a free clinic with social services where she is also willing to lend them a hand."

Sarah gave him another winning smile. "Time's up, Officer Miller, is there a downside to this whole crazy mess as you see it?"

Cady smiled back. "Well Ms. Mitchell, I see your conviction rate going down, both today and in the future if they don't become repeat offenders."

Sarah laughed out loud. "Let me think on this and get back to you. I'll want to interview both boys and their mother before I decide."

"Fair enough," Cady said, extending his big hand across the desk.

~

Back with Red in the squad car by 9:30 they checked in with the duty sergeant then hit the streets. Cady brought Red up to speed on the meeting and asked for his opinion.

"You live it, don't you?" Red asked his partner. "You really buy into it and walk the walk."

Cady shrugged and hesitated. "Try to. I grew up without a dad. I know what it is like."

Red continued, "What did John say when you asked him? How'd he take it?"

Cady smiled then answered, "Haven't yet."

John was standing outside when they pulled up at the Blue Canoe. Cady left Red to mind the car and gave the desk sergeant his 10-20 before going inside. The chiefs were already seated with a third man. Cady introduced himself and John to the guest and thanked the chiefs for taking the time to meet. Cady's chief was content to let Jordan carry the ball and only spoke up from time to time to clarify or answer questions.

Johnson was FBI and part of the task force working on leads concerning the terrorist threat. As part of an ongoing surveillance on a suspected cell in Montreal, Canada, the FBI had stopped and arrested three Syrian nationals who were attempting to cross the border into the U.S. under the false floor of their mini van. In the sub-frame of the van was over a hundred pounds of plastic explosives. The three were being held incognito in an agreement with the Canadian government.

Finally they understand that something is going on, that these several incidents are part of something bigger, Cady thought. *And finally they have enough evidence to move on it.*

He asked Johnson straight out, "What is the game plan now that you have enough proof to get your bosses' attention?"

Johnson began with the party line statement just as he would have given the press, "We are taking all possible precautions, investigating every lead, and have all probable targets under close scrutiny."

"Yeah, right," John commented. "Have any of the suspects offered up information in addition to the one Cady outsmarted?"

"Well no, not at this time," Johnson answered. "But we are hopeful ..."

Cady interrupted, "Hopeful of what? That the damage will not be significant, that there will be few casualties, that you can hang it on another department for dropping the ball?" Cady was seldom angry but at the moment he was enraged, having pushed and pushed just to get them to have minds open enough to investigate.

Chief Jordan interceded in an attempt to keep the conversation civil, "Have you constructive solutions to offer, Officer Miller?"

It was a gentle rebuff, but Cady knew he had overstepped. "Yes, and no, sir. Meaning I don't claim to know all the answers, but I am committed to looking for them. Mr. Johnson, you, the CIA, NSA, or someone must certainly have infiltrated some of the local Islamic community. Are you without credible intel from them?"

Johnson began, "I am not at liberty ..."

Jordan cut him off, "You certainly are at liberty to say, and say now. Need I get the mayor, the governor, and the commissioner on the phone?"

Johnson began again, "What I should have said is that what we have has not been substantiated."

"Understood!" Jordan thundered. "Now tell us what unsubstantiated information you do have."

Johnson began to perspire. "We actually have leads that suggest a three-pronged attack. One, all or none of these may be accurate. First, a suicide bombing or substantial detonation of explosives in one or more locations. Due to the explosives already in custody this seems the most likely. Second, there is a suggestion that the explosives may be used in conjunction with a biological or chemical agent in our underground transportation systems. And finally, the possibility of the use of aircraft presenting a more visual assault to our vulnerability being showcased before the world."

The room fell quiet.

Finally Jordan resumed the floor. "Thank you for your candid report. May I ask how the administration is viewing this threat?"

Johnson smiled for the first time. "You may ask, but you'll get no subjective answer from me. But in a word, seriously. Anything more is way above my pay grade. One more thing, and keep it in this room please. What we have is not all new news. It began in the last administration and has grown and become more real in the new one. They have had time to plan and implement, design and redesign the assault over several years. It just now seems to be culminating. In effect they have cried wolf so many times we had let our guard down.

The men present were skilled and intelligent men. They could see the wisdom in the agent's statement. They could also see why it could never become general public knowledge. Americans, unlike many other nations' citizens, had never had to live in fear. God, geography, power and money had always served to make them feel secure and invulnerable.

Cady thought back on Red's words of wisdom after the taxi-bomb incident, *Welcome to a world gone mad.*

When the meeting broke up, John walked Cady to the cruiser where Red sat waiting. They shook hands but said little. It was ominous and too big to consider possible. Cady promised to call him later in the evening.

"Well?" Red said in the form of a question. "Did you get a promotion?"

Cady had to smile. "Probably not, but they may let me keep my job."

They checked in with the precinct before resuming a non-eventful afternoon shift.

Introspective was a word that almost perfectly described Cady's demeanor at home that evening. Withdrawn, was the word Shawna used when finally tiring of his lack of family involvement and one-word answers to their questions. The girls picked up on it first and asked their mom if he was feeling well. Each of the girls wondered what they might have done to cause the change in his usual pleasant disposition.

Remote was how Cady felt – distant, overwhelmed, without a plan or energy to implement one. That he couldn't share with the love of his life the true story and was unwilling to make one up made conversation difficult. Rather than call John, Cady excused himself saying that he needed to make a visit. He did not offer that any might join him.

Cady left, knowing that he needed someone with whom he could talk openly. John seemed the right choice. When he arrived, John was waiting and Helen was already on the phone with Shawna. The two men each grabbed a beer and went to the RV where they could talk. At first they said little, skirting the real issue, unwilling to admit their fears.

Inside the two veteran wives talked openly, sharing information and questioning the meaning of the changes in their husbands. Helen had known of the meeting with Chief Jordan, but of course not its purpose. Shawna had not. As they pieced it together it became clear that the meeting was the cause of their husbands' discontent, leaving the unanswered questions: What was the purpose of the meeting? And what could change both men's personalities so drastically and so quickly?

Cady was the first to break the ice. "I've seldom felt so helpless and alone. The more I try and think through this the more out of control I feel. I just can't seem to get my head around all of this."

John nodded, then said, "Likewise my friend, the implications are overwhelming. I am so glad you came over. I needed so badly to share with someone but could not."

Cady nodded.

John continued, "There is One with whom we can share, One who knows our deepest fears, who already knows what the future holds."

Cady nodded again. *Why hadn't he thought to pray? Who more than God is able to calm our fears, to give us clarity and wisdom, the strength to endure no matter what does happen?*

Both men knelt and prayed aloud. After several minutes they stopped, feeling emotionally drained but infilled with God's Holy Spirit. Neither spoke for several moments, reveling in their newly found peace.

It was Cady who spoke first. "What a peace I feel. The fear is gone, but I still have no answers for my questions."

"Likewise," John said. "I still cannot see what path to take or what I should do next, but I feel comfortable to let God's plan just happen."

A knock on the door interrupted their discussion. It was Helen.

John opened the door and welcomed her in with a smile. "Come in and join us, Honey."

A surprised look replaced the worried one on her face as she sat next to him. It was Helen's turn to speak. "What have you boys been up to?"

Avoiding the specifics Cady said, "Just talking and praying together, not much else."

John nodded and smiled. "We needed to move up close to the Lord and feel His presence. We were both feeling kind of out of touch with Him."

The answers seemed to satisfy her curiosity but didn't answer her questions. She smiled then said, "How about joining me for coffee and cookies?"

Both men returned the smile and followed her toward the house. By the time Cady walked in the door Helen and Shawna had enjoyed another conversation. Both were pleased with the results of the men's time together but curious of what had precipitated the need for it. Neither Cady nor John were asked directly or volunteered anything, so the matter just faded away.

Five

As he arrived for his shift, Cady received a note from the desk sergeant that had the name Sarah Mitchell followed by her number. He could almost see her smile and freckles that gave her nose the look of a child who had played in the sandbox too long.

She picked up her phone, no doubt noting the number on her caller ID. "Well, big guy you made a good case for the Brown boys and the mother too. I'm willing to give them a chance. I've set up a meeting with the judge and the public defender for tomorrow to plead your case to him. I'd like you and John to join us in case he has any questions or stipulations. Can you make two o'clock?"

Cady cringed then answered, "Let me give John a call and get back to you." *Why didn't I bring the subject up yesterday when we were together? Oh well, as grandma used to say, "The fat's in the fire."*

~

"Morning Helen, Cady here. Is John around?" he asked.

"Sure, right here. I'll get him," she answered.

Cady looked heavenward, took a deep breath, and opened his mouth to speak.

"Morning Cady, expecting your call. How you feelin' this fine morning?" John said cheerily.

Cady sensed a lightness in his voice and a bit of humor too. "Fine John, thanks for asking, and you?"

"Fine as frog hair," came the chuckled reply. "What's on your mind my friend?" Before Cady could answer, John continued, "Hey you remember that little freckled redhead in the DA's office? Just hung up talking with her. She had one heck of an idea. Want to hear about it?"

While John and Helen were about to burst their stitches, Cady was dying inside. "Sure John, I remember her." He almost whispered, "What did she have to say?"

"Said I needed to meet with you tomorrow at two o'clock with Judge Baines. Something about doing some public service," John said laughing out loud.

"I'm sorry, John," Cady offered. "I meant to ask you, but we got caught up in the meeting with the chief and I forgot. Please forgive me. I'm trying hard to help these boys and you were the first one I thought of."

John was still laughing at the picture of Cady squirming on the line when he said, "Turns out, I had a cancelation in my busy schedule giving me a slot open at two o'clock tomorrow. See you there." He didn't give Cady further opportunity to grovel before hanging up.

~

John showed up at roll call just like when he served. This time, however, with several dozen fresh donuts under his arm. Needless to say he was warmly greeted. He asked and received permission from the watch commander to do a ride-along with Red and Cady.

Once on the streets he opened the conversation, "Tell me, Cady, where are we going with this meeting with the DA?"

Cady began at the beginning describing the shooting, their pursuit, the take down and arrest, and the subsequent information that led him to champion for the brothers. He also said that he had implied that John would be a participant in mentoring the two.

John's deep, rich laugh echoed in the closed compartment, "Implied, implied? The little redhead said you had all the details worked out. Is Shawna a willing victim too?"

Cady mumbled, "Yes, I did mention it to her."

Still messing with him, John continued, "And she's on board with it? Has she met with them, interviewed their mother, considered what a time investment it could be?"

Cady was finally done taking his beating. "She works with kids like this all the time. She knows better than me."

John's voice turned cheery, "Helen loves the idea. She wants me to get another horse to keep at your place so you can teach them how to ride. Did you say they are Christian boys?"

Cady responded, "Yes, I think so. Both they and their mother said as much."

"Hmm, I wonder if the three would like to join us Sunday."

Cady nodded. "Let's just get past the hearing and see how things go first."

John let the subject drop.

At ten o'clock Cady bought them coffee while waiting for their first incident. The squawk finally came. It was a 10-10, a fight in progress, near the middle school just around the corner. Drawing a large crowd, it was the kind of thing that could turn bad quickly if gang members were involved. As they pulled up, several faded into the background while others stood their places casting belligerent looks at the black and white.

Two boys, in their early teens and about evenly matched in size, were mixing it up on the ground with no visible weapons.

Cady walked up, joined the circle, and asked one of the onlookers, "Who's winnin'?"

Surprise showed in the boy's face at the question, expecting the uniforms to jump in to action. "Joe was at first, but that's Bill on top now. Hard to say."

Cady nodded before asking, "They fight a lot, Joe and Bill?"

"Nope, never," came the reply. "They're best friends."

Joe rolled Bill off and was trying to get to his feet. The circle urged them on. Bill was red faced, beginning to show the strain of battle, but trying hard to look determined to the crowd. Cady guessed them about thirteen or fourteen, both a shade over five feet, and pushing 110 to 115 pounds.

Cady turned back to the onlooker, "Why they fightin' now?"

He laughed before responding. "They both think Mary Ellen likes them, but she doesn't. She likes Blake Smith."

Cady nearly laughed with him. "Is Blake here?"

"Yeah, that's him over there," he said pointing to a taller boy in a red T-shirt.

"And Mary Ellen," Cady continued. "Where is she?"

"Right there by Blake, got her arm in his," the informant said.

Red and John stood nearby waiting for instruction from Cady. He walked over to them and brought them up to speed, noticing that the combatants were winded but trying stubbornly to hold onto their pride.

Cady turned to Red and John with a twinkle in his eye. "Let's arrest them and take them for ice cream."

Red smiled broadly as he and Cady grabbed the boys roughly, before producing handcuffs. "Shall we cuff 'em 'fore we take 'em away?" he said to Cady.

"Better," Cady answered. "They've already shown they're ready to fight."

Cuffed in front, the two were pushed into the backseat, one on either side of John. The crowd stood abuzz as the cruiser pulled onto the street with lights and siren.

Red leaned toward the backseat. "Sorry boys, we don't normally put juvies in with hard cases like John here, but we could see you meant to kill each other. Had to get you off the street. We were taking him to the courthouse when we got the call."

John sneered at them. "I got a date with the judge at two o'clock. Maybe we can share a cell sometime."

Cady got into the act. "Who's this Blake guy who got away with your girl? He a tough too?"

Joe said almost inaudibly, "He's a ninth grader, thinks he's a big deal."

"Yeah," Bill added. "She only knows him from study hall. She's in seventh like us."

"Wouldn't be the first time two guys killed each other over a woman, then she ran off with a stranger," John said. "I've seen it before."

The boys fell silent.

"We weren't gonna kill anyone," Bill said. We just got to shovin' each other. Then the crowd came around and pretty soon we couldn't quit."

Cady spied a Baskin-Robbins ahead on the right so he slowed. "That right?" he asked. "You're not trying to kill each other?"

"No, sir," was their simultaneous reply.

"We've been best friends since fourth grade," said Joe.

Cady hit his mic, "We have the suspects in custody. We're going to be 10-35 at 10421 Lamont for a few minutes to interrogate the suspects."

The address of course was the ice cream shop, well known to many of New York's finest.

Cady pulled the cruiser to the curb, a few doors from their ultimate destination, then shut off the ignition.

Looking at the boys he said, "Boys, there are few things in life more valuable than friendships. You will come to know that and appreciate it more and more the older you get. Friendship is a form of love – of the love that Jesus wants us to have for each other. It's different than what you feel for your family, or may one day feel for your wife and children, but love all the same. It is something to be cherished. It is more valuable than money. There could come a day when you might have to choose a friend's life over your own. If you have that love you won't even hesitate, just as my Savior Jesus did not hesitate to die for me so that I could live. Do you know Jesus, who He is and how much He loves you?"

The boys both looked down not answering.

Red joined the conversation. "You should. He will help you make the right decisions so that your lives will be worth living."

They dropped the conversation and went inside where they enjoyed double dippers together. Cady left the cuffs on while they ate, just for effect, then took them off and drove the boys back to the school yard. Red and Ben delivered them to the resource officer with a wink preferring to let the school mete out any necessary punishment.

It had been an interesting morning protecting and serving. Cady prayed silently for God's intervention in their upcoming meeting with ADA Mitchell and Judge Baines. When he and John entered the judge's chambers at ten o'clock, Ted and Tom, their mother, Sarah Mitchell, the public defender and the judge were already seated.

The judge smiled at John. "Gentlemen, why are we hear today?"

Cady stood and started to speak but closed his mouth and reseated himself when he saw the judge looking at the boys. The pause was deafening as the judge waited for the two young men to respond.

Finally understanding the question was not going away, Tom stood. "Because, sir, Ted and I messed up big time."

Cady nodded. It was a good start, taking responsibility for their mistakes.

"And you, Son?" the judge asked turning toward the younger brother whose eyes were rimmed with tears.

"Sir, judge," Ted began tentatively, "it was all my fault. Tom wouldn't have been there at all if I had not decided to skip school."

Their mother was nodding her head.

"Do you skip school often?" the judge asked him quietly.

"No, sir," came the joint response immediately.

"First time this year," Ted added.

"And last year?" the judge asked gently.

"We cut class early one time when the school was in the championship game."

"Are you on the team?" the judge continued, sounding interested in how they conducted themselves on a day-by-day basis.

"No, sir," they both admitted.

"That was varsity, we are just JV."

Judge Baines continued, "A little short for varsity. You a shootin' guard?"

"No," Ted admitted. "Tom is, I'm the off guard."

Judge Baines was a tall black man, in his mid-fifties, with salt and pepper in his curly hair, and tall enough to have played basketball.

"Mrs. Brown," the judge said, " I have visited with the prosecutor at length about your sons but would like to hear from you about why we should be sitting here today rather than just going into the courtroom. Where is the boys' father?"

Mrs. Brown retold the story just as she had to Cady, and probably Sarah as well. Apparently Sarah had not repeated it to the judge, thinking it would be more effective coming directly from her. She was a humble woman but held her head high with a certain enviable dignity as she summarized their lives. Baines nodded and from time to time asked for clarification from her.

Then in a change of tact, he asked her bluntly, "Who do you blame for the mess they are in?"

To her credit, she didn't rattle easily. She seemed to think for a moment before answering, "I don't blame no one 'cept them. I always taught them to take responsibility for themselves and learn from their mistakes."

Good answer, thought Cady noticing at the pensive look on the judge's face.

"Officer Miller," the judge said while returning Cady's gaze, "what made you throw your hat into the ring here?" Cady stood, but before he could speak the judge continued, "Aren't you the arresting officer? Wasn't this boy running down the street carrying a weapon?"

Cady hadn't expected this but also took time to compose his answers. "Yes, my partner and I arrested these young men. And yes, Ted was armed with a weapon used in a shooting a few blocks away."

Baines nodded but did not speak.

Cady continued, "Why did I choose to get involved is a big question. After interviewing each boy, talking with their mother, and praying for God's guidance, I feel that it is part of my pledge to protect and serve. I feel these boys are at a crossroad, this being a defining moment in their young lives. I feel a debt to their fallen father for his service that I may in part repay."

"Are you a crusader, Miller? Are you one of those who's looking to fix a broken world?"

Cady looked him in the eyes. "Maybe yes, maybe I am to some effect. I had never thought of it that way. I don't go looking for causes, but when I see something where I might make a difference, I do try and fix it."

At this Baines smiled broadly. "Well said, Officer."

"Now you, John," the judge said as to an old friend. "How'd you get involved in all this? I thought you were retired."

John smiled at him. "I am retired but not by choice. I still have a few good years left in me, God willing. My partner here needed backup. You know how that works. When a friend calls you are there for him."

"And these boys?" the judge asked. "Who are they to you?"

"Never laid eyes on them," came his honest reply. "But if they are willing to accept my help, I'm willing to try. Comes with the territory, Judge. You can't be a Christian just when it suits you or when you are helping someone you already care about. You've gotta love everyone the same way Jesus loves us. I figure I owe them a chance."

"ADA Mitchell, anything to add?" the judge asked looking at Sarah.

"I do have a plan that I believe serves the interest of the community while allowing the suspects a chance to reclaim their futures," Sarah said, placing several papers on the judge's desk.

"Let me look over your proposal and have an answer for you in the morning."

"Boys," he said looking at each with a piercing stare, "if I grant this request it will be the first in all my years on the bench. This might be a good time to get on your knees and pray."

Cady's heart fell with the judge's last statement. Up to that point he had felt things were going well, that there was chance. Now, he wanted to re-plead the case, give it another try, be as eloquent and cleaver as he had been with Mitchell. He felt he had let the boys down, advocated poorly for them.

~

Back in the cruiser the men remained quiet while Red drove.

"He's a fair man. Most wouldn't have taken the time to listen at all," John offered, speaking mostly to himself. "That's good advice he gave the boys. I think all of us would do well to lift the situation up to the Lord."

Cady nodded, but had already given up, despair flooding over him. The judge had the final say and he had never said yes.

Later at the station, John took time to reacquaint with old friends while Cady and Red filed their dailies.

Six

Cady came home in another dour mood. He hardly took the time to visit with his family before he went out to his workshop. In fifteen minutes he was back at the house with a paper towel around his hand. He was muttering under his breath as blood soaked through the paper towel. Shawna washed and dressed the wound and attempted to draw him into conversation. The girls joined them, full of questions and excess energy. "AWANA is tonight and we are working with the Sparkies. Will you come and help Dad?" they asked.

"Not tonight," he answered a little too loudly. "I need some time alone."

Shawna looked up at him in surprise but chose to say nothing as the girls disappeared like water vapor. They had dinner together without the usual banter and bickering between the twins. Somehow it seemed food without conversation didn't taste as good.

"No, John," Cady said into the phone, "not tonight. I don't really feel like a Bible study."

John was adept at reading people from his years of practice on the streets. He replied, "So you thought I didn't have anything to do today except go to court? I came because you asked me. You are my friend. Now I'm asking you to come and join me."

Cady had no way out but to agree, but it ticked him off as well that John would use their friendship for his own benefit.

~

When they arrived at the church, the chairs were drawn into a circle with several men already seated. The topic for the evening was learning dependence upon God. Pastor Orville opened in prayer asking God to open ears and hearts to His Word. They discussed man's necessary dependency upon God. The debate went on for some time before they closed with Orville asking if there were needs or burdens among the group that needed prayer. Several spoke of illnesses, financial considerations, and employment situations. Cady remained silent, not engaging actively, then moved off by himself as the men paired up.

A young man, who he had never met, approached him. "My name is Solomon," he said sticking out his hand. "Most call me Sol. I am new to this church, a converted Jew."

Cady was intrigued by the young man, having never personally met or known a Jew. He found himself looking at the boy, appraising his nose, the color of his skin, his hair.

Sol noticed Cady's scrutiny. "Am I what you expected?"

Cady was embarrassed, unable to find an appropriate answer. Finally he recovered enough to speak. "I am sorry I was so blatant. I have never met or known a Jewish person. I guess I was curious if one could tell by appearance."

Sol laughed. "The truth is that Judaism is both a nationality and a religion, which confuses many. Then, like in America, several races are involved. We go from fair skinned to black, light hair to dark, small stature to large. Did you know that there were giants, actual giants in Gath? Goliath of David was one of those, though not a Jew."

Cady smiled.

Sol continued, "Most people look at the odd, little men dressed funny with large noses and olive skin as stereotypical."

Cady actually laughed, knowing that is exactly what he had expected.

"I am told King Solomon, for who I was named, was a large man with blond hair. Although he was chosen by God Himself, he turned out to be a disappointment in the end, as we all must be to God. Now King David was more the typical size and coloring that one might expect from a full-blooded Jew."

Again Cady laughed, wondering where all this was going.

"There is much debate at how many of the twelve apostles were dark skinned from North Africa," Sol continued.

By now Cady had forgotten the dark cloud that had engulfed him since leaving the courthouse. "What do you do, I mean what kind of work do you do?" Cady asked.

"What I am told," he answered with conviction. "Right now I am engaging you and wondering how I can help you."

Cady was uncertain as how to answer or what exactly the young man had meant. "Does it show?" Cady asked. "I mean does it show that I am conflicted?"

"It is apparent that you are having a crisis of faith," he answered.

"Crisis of faith? What exactly does that mean?" Cady said with some emotion. "And how would you know if I were?"

"It is apparent that you are burdened and should turn to God for help in lightening your load. Often we forget that He is the answer to all questions, the solution to all problems."

Cady had been looking across the room where John was visiting with Orville while the young man spoke. When he turned his attention back to the young visitor he was gone. Looking around the room he was nowhere to be seen. *Impossible*, Cady thought to himself. *Five seconds ago we were debating, and he was offering help. Now he is gone?*

After several more seconds Cady walked over to where Orville and John were talking. When they noticed him standing nearby they greeted him warmly.

"About time you joined us instead of standing in the corner by yourself," John said.

Cady ignored his comment, turned to the pastor and asked, "Pastor Orville, can you tell me anything about the new guy that I was talking to? The young Jew convert named Sol."

Both men looked at him questioningly.

"Sol? Converted Jew? What are you talking about?"

Cady felt a chill, an odd sensation down his back and legs. He wondered if he was losing his mind. Smiling, Cady took a different route, "So neither of you saw me talking with a young man? You didn't notice a new guy in the Bible study tonight?"

John looked alarmed. "Are you okay partner? I mean do you feel okay? I am sorry to have twisted your arm to come tonight when you said you didn't feel up to it."

Orville asked, "Where was the young man sitting in Bible study? Perhaps I missed welcoming him."

Cady thought but try as he might he could not remember. All seats had been filled, he remembered. But which one held Sol? He did not know.

John was looking at him oddly. Taking charge he addressed the crowd, "Gentlemen, would everyone take your seat again for a few minutes?"

Conversation stopped as they returned to the chairs and sat down. Cady looked around the circle for his new friend in vain. Every seat was filled.

There were tears running down Cady's cheeks when he began to speak. "Brothers, I have a confession to make before you and before God." He slowly told every detail of the pursuit, arrest, questioning, and his plan for the rehabilitation of the two young men. Then he related the conversation at the courthouse and his great disappointment when he and John had left that meeting. Finally, he told of the great weight of despair he carried with him, even to the study tonight. Then he told word for word the conversation he shared with Sol.

There was an uneasy quiet in the room as each man had personal revelation of the event that had just happened.

There was a sense of awe with little conversation when Orville said, "Gentlemen perhaps we have been privileged to have been in the presence of an angel this evening. It seems only fitting that we turn to God in prayer and ask Him for guidance and direction. Cady would you start us off?"

Overcome with emotion, Cady struggled to speak through his tears. He asked for God's forgiveness, thanked Him for His special provision, and sought guidance and direction in all matters, especially in the matter of the Brown boys. He continued on until he was emotionally spent, seeing Sol's young face before him the whole time. One by one each man moved toward the Lord spiritually, speaking from the heart, and appreciating the feeling of reverent contrition. When Orville finally closed there was a sacred silence before each man rose and left for home.

As they drove home John and Cady did not converse, rather content to contemplate the events of the evening. There was a peace in Cady's heart he hadn't felt since accepting Jesus.

~

Shawna looked at him when he opened the door, and asked, "You feelin' better? Was the study good tonight?"

Cady answered, "Yes, and yes, it was wonderful. I need some sleep right now, but I want to tell you all about it tomorrow."

Sleep enfolded him like soft cotton, with the vision of Sol's face fading away finally as he lost consciousness. His last thought was the hope that he'd never forget tonight. *I can do all this through Him who strengthens me* was the verse on his mind when he awoke to the sound of giggling coming from the kitchen. Shawna was cooking Dutch babies, a combination between a pancake and scone, one of the family's favorites. After each was cooked they were topped with fresh strawberries, whipped cream and powdered sugar, and link sausage on the side. When Cady entered the kitchen the giggling stopped abruptly as the children assessed his mood. He felt guilt and sorrow that he'd made them feel they had to test the water before they could proceed by his poor behavior the previous night.

His smile restored their faith in him. He couldn't remember when he had slept so well and felt so rested. After they wolfed down the first bites and settled into their seats he said, "I have something to say." There was a look of uncertainty before he continued, "I want to apologize to each of you for the way I acted last night. And, though I have no excuse, I want to share with you some things regarding the two boys we talked about earlier."

Cady went briefly back over the details of the pursuit, capture, jailing and interrogation.

He then offered them the information that he had decided to try and help the boys, to which the girls rolled their eyes and said, "Of course."

He told about the meeting with the ADA and the later one that he and Uncle John had with the judge. He admitted that he had felt it necessary and his responsibility to make it all work out according to his plan. Again their eyes rolled. This time Shawna joined in but did not interrupt. That brought him to last night and his plea for their forgiveness and God's forgiveness for doubting His love and care.

Cady emphasized that he, like all men, sometimes tries and assume God's role. Feeling independent and proud, he tries to make events happen without God's blessings.

There was not a sound in the room as everyone nodded in agreement. They stopped eating, each enwrapped in the unfolding adventure.

"Now" he said, pausing for effect, "the really cool stuff." He told how he felt when John had invited him to Bible study, how he went from a sense of duty but without interest, how he disdained from contributing to the discussion, and finally he told them about Sol. In every detail, remembering every word and nuance, describing his every feeling, and finally the peace he felt last night and still today. As he relived it, tears returned to his eyes and emotions filled him once again. It became hard for him to continue speaking.

The kitchen remained quiet for several minutes as everyone absorbed the enormity of what they had heard.

Finally, with a twinkle in her brown eyes, Faith asked, "So was he cute?"

As usual she brought down the house. Cady pretended to chase her to punish her as she ran and squealed. The twins laughed gleefully

Seven

It was Friday morning, his last duty day for the week, when he pulled up at the house with Red right behind him.

They stood roll call, got their assignments, and were headed toward their car when the desk sergeant stopped them. "Miller, I've got another message for you. You got something going on with the redhead at the DA's office?" he joked.

Cady winked as he pocketed the note, "Yeah something."

In the car Red took shotgun while Cady took the wheel.

"How'd it go yesterday," he asked Cady, referring to the meeting.

Cady thought before responding. "Well, yesterday I'd have told you that I wasted my time. Today I hope to find out that we won the war."

When they stopped for a coffee break Cady made the call.

"Mitchell speaking," was Sarah's greeting, having not recognized Cady's cell number.

Cady tried to keep it light while holding his breath as though it might make a difference. "Cady here, you called?"

"Yes! Yes, Blaine left me a message at home last night regarding the Brown case." She stopped speaking for a moment for effect. "He said we'd better not make him sorry, that he was willing to give them a chance. But he emphasized that if he sees them in his court again, you and I better not be living in New York state."

"So," Cady said happily, "we won?"

"No, stupid, you won, they won. I lost," Sarah said with mock pain in her voice. "My batting average just went down a point. We've got to get together and work out the details on this. I don't want it to blow up in our faces."

Cady was smiling ear to ear. *Thank you God*, he thought to himself.

"How about over dinner?" Cady said jokingly. Before she could answer or wonder at his intentions, he continued, "We need to have John, Helen and Shawna there too. Later we can include the Brown family and go over our expectations and rules with them. That sound okay? I'll touch base with everyone today and see if we can find a convenient time to meet."

Sarah nodded through the phone then said, "Yes, please get back to me."

Cady first called Shawna. She was open timewise and was looking forward to meeting the two boys.

Next he called John and Helen answered. "Hi Cady. Heard you had an interesting evening last night."

Cady smiled remembering. "Interesting doesn't do it justice," he replied. "What's the word I'm looking for, epiphany?"

"Don't know," she teased. "Can you spell it for me?"

"I doubt it. Is John nearby?"

"Yes, I'll call him."

When John came to the phone Cady asked if he might have Helen pick up a phone also so he could speak with them both. Cady did a poor job of hiding his excitement as he told them of Sarah's call and the need for a brainstorming session. "May I buy you dinner tomorrow evening?" Cady said. "Shawna and Sarah Mitchell will join us also?"

"How about Red?" John asked, surprising Cady.

"Red? Do you think he needs to be involved in it?"

"Already is, seems to me," the older officer replied. "Has been from the start. Didn't you say he made a connection with one of the boys at the hospital?"

"Yes, he did," Cady said, remembering how Red had prayed with Ted. "Good idea. Let me visit with him this afternoon and see what he says. So is five o'clock good for you? Shawna and I could pick you up and visit on the way into town?"

They agreed. "Bring your credit card big boy, this is going to cost you plenty."

Cady laughed with them. "It's God's money. It's easy to spend someone else's money."

Next he called Marshall's, one of Shawna's favorite restaurants and made reservations at seven o'clock for six. Then he called the DA's office and left a message for Sarah who was back in court.

Cady and Red responded to a 10-18, a hold up at a local bodega, and arrived after the suspect had fled with a small amount of money.

The owner of the mom and pop store had not recognized the perp as a local, but gave a good description and identified the weapon as a .25 auto. "A woman's gun," he said with disdain.

They collected scant evidence but did locate a possible witness who had seen the suspect flee the store. She confirmed the description and the fact that he was not from the hood. When the detectives arrived Cady gave them what they had gathered then introduced them to the witness before leaving.

Back in the cruiser, Cady turned to his partner and asked, "You busy tomorrow night?"

Red looked at him quizzically before answering, "No plans that I can't change. What's on your mind?"

"Dinner," Cady said matter-of-factly. "Gonna have dinner at Marshall's with a few friends and go over the Brown case together. You interested?"

"You buyin'?" the younger officer asked. "I heard they have sweeeet food but a bit above my budget."

"I'm buyin'. Can you be there by seven o'clock?"

"With bells on," Red said with enthusiasm. "Do I have to order off the kids menu?"

Cady didn't answer, just shook his head and took the squawk that came over the radio. It was another holdup a few blocks away, this one still in progress, called in by witnesses. Cady and Red took the call asking dispatch to relay the call to the two detectives investigating the first robbery.

With lights on but no sirens they sped through traffic, stopping purposely a few doors away behind a delivery truck. The truck obscured the black and white from their view of the store, while at the same time the perp's view of them. Cady called dispatch with their 20 then asked Red to take up a position across the street, keeping out of sight while maintaining a visual of the front of the store. He grabbed the 12-gauge from its mount and checked its breech for a shell before stepping onto the sidewalk. Foot traffic on the sidewalk ahead of him disappeared at his appearance. He took a squawk on his shoulder unit from the detectives en route giving them the lay of the land and asking that they approach from the other side to help with foot traffic control. Suddenly

Sol came to mind, his face distinct in Cady's memory. Cady stopped and prayed for God's direction and help in resolving the situation. The face was gone.

Cady stepped into the recess of the doorway entrance next to the store, hoping that the perp would exit with the cash without using his weapon as he had before. If Cady entered, those inside would likely become hostages or worse when he confronted the suspect. There was always a chance that no matter which he chose the situation could escalate into a shooting. He prayed the owner would give over the money without conflict and allow the man to flee into his waiting arms.

Pop, pop! No such luck. Two shots were fired from a small caliber weapon. Cady was now being forced to enter the shop. But before he could, a tall, heavy black man came stumbling out the front holding his bleeding head with one hand, a gun in the other. Cady took out his inside knee with the butt of the 12-gauge, causing the giant to fall toward the storefront. As the man fell, Cady pressed the "business end" of the weapon against his bleeding skull.

"Drop your weapon," Cady said.

All at once Red and the two detectives were there, kicking the .25 away, cuffing and rolling the man onto his back. Cady was up and inside the store where he found the storekeeper standing, still holding a baseball bat, while bleeding from two chest wounds.

The EMTs came on the scene. They had to force the old crusader to lie down on the stretcher.

"BP good, vitals good, loss of blood minimal," Cady heard them report.

Over his objections they took him away after waiting for his wife to come down and secure the store. Later Cady found out that the shopkeeper had been a prisoner of war in Vietnam for seven years before escaping. Today's ordeal must have seemed trivial to such a man. The small caliber weapon had not even penetrated his sternum, being stopped before entering the chest cavity where it would have seriously injured or killed him. Cady would have bet money that he'd have returned to work the same day if they released him.

When Cady stepped onto the sidewalk, the two detectives were assisting their suspect into yet another ambulance for a ride to the hospital to treat his broken knee.

Red seemed angry when Cady approached him. "A lot of nerve they have stealing our arrest," he said. "They showed up just in time to use their handcuffs."

Cady smiled, remembering when he had taken personal pride in his arrest record also. "Well," Cady said with a grin, "they bought themselves a load of paperwork and probably a trial appearance on their day off. I figure we got the best of the deal."

Red, who seemed appeased at the thought of them working overtime, smiled too.

~

Cady picked Shawna up at the clinic, which allowed them time to unwind before arriving home. They were lucky enough to ride together once or twice a week and enjoyed their alone time together. There it is again, 'alone together.' You've got to wonder how that happens.

She told of her day ministering to the heart of a thirteen-year-old, pregnant Puerto Rican girl, who was angry and scared. Shawna suspected sexual abuse at home but had no proof as yet to support her theory. Her mother was living with a man who had access to the children while she was at work.

Cady listened then asked, "Will she try and keep the child?"

"I hope not," came Shawna's reply. "They have five already in a two-bedroom rent-controlled apartment plus the live-in boyfriend. The mother is the only one working with the system barely keeping them afloat. I hope she will allow adoption."

Cady nodded, "Does she see that as an option?"

"No, at this point she wants an abortion. She actually hates the child within her. That is why I suspect rape or sexual abuse."

When they got home Cady went out to the barn with his daughters. He took the twins into his arms and held them close, offering silent thanks for them. They were about to turn fourteen. Faith, nearly fifteen, watched but said nothing waiting for her turn to feel a father's love.

Isn't that what we all want, to feel a father's love, he thought, as they brushed out the coats of the two horses in their barn. Their horses were rescue horses, impounded from their owners for protection from abuse. They were six now and full grown, two small geldings from the same mare. Cady guessed they had they been treated and fed well they'd both have been larger and more active. As it was, they were still timid and hesitant unable to fully trust in humans, even after three years of loving care with the Miller family. *Another lesson there*, Cady thought to himself, *only He is trustworthy and true.*

Shawna called from the house. "Cady, it's Chief Jordan."

"Yes, Chief," Cady said, having taken the receiver from Shawna. "Yes, I understand. Yes, we plan to be in town tomorrow evening, but I could come in earlier if necessary. Yes, John and Helen are coming with us also for dinner. Yes, let me ask them and call you back. Thank you, goodbye."

Shawna had heard only Cady's side of the conversation and was curious, so she asked, "Trouble?"

Cady knew he had to walk carefully, answering her honestly but not fully. "John and I are working with the chief on a very important, but not public, task force. We think it might be tied to our shootings in July and hope that it may lead somewhere. But we are not at liberty to share details with anyone." He emphasized the word anyone, hoping she might not pursue the matter further. "He wondered if John and I might meet with him tomorrow when we are in town. It might give you and Helen a chance to do some shopping if you are up to it." Cady knew that she knew he was offering her a carrot so she would drop the discussion.

Smiling, she wisely but knowingly took the bait. "When did two women ever pass up a chance to shop before going out to a fancy dinner? Why don't you let me call Helen?"

Having visited with Helen for an hour, Shawna turned to Cady and said, "It's all set. You can tell the chief that we are picking them up at noon tomorrow for lunch on our way in."

When Cady called Jordan back they set up a meet for three o'clock at the chief's office.

Having given their daughters a list of chores, emergency phone numbers, and a volume of instructions as to handle every imaginable situation that might arise, Shawna and Cady pulled their sedan from the gravel driveway. It was not often that they left them alone, and then only for a few hours, seldom a full day. They both had misgivings and fears but neither shared their angst. Privately they prayed for God's protection over their most precious possession.

The mood changed when John and Helen joined them. The conversation became light and frivolous with the women using the leverage of the meetings to their advantage. They hit an IHOP before leaving the outskirts of the city where the men enjoyed breakfast and the women had French dip sandwiches and fries. It was just after two o'clock when they entered the metropolis with its skyline touching the clouds. It was always a thrill to the Millers, the first sight of the big city, and a relief when they left it behind.

"Where first?" Cady asked, speaking to the two women and remembering their threat to shop 'til they dropped. Finally the women chose a medium-priced boutique in the middle of the clothing district with off street parking. The men were silent but rolled their eyes trying to imitate the women from memory. Of course they got caught in the act receiving many verbal threats of retribution for the unseemly act.

"We'll call when the meeting is finished and set up a rendezvous," Cady said trying to sound practical and efficient.

"Right," Shawna said smiling. "You call and we'll let you know where to pick us up."

"Isn't that what I just said?" Cady directed at John.

It felt strange to park in visitor's parking, so Cady nosed the sedan into a police only spot at the station house, hung his photo ID over the rearview mirror, and locked the doors. Still a few minutes early, they helped themselves to coffee and visited with the duty shift. The 26th was unremarkable, looking much the same as the 23rd where Cady hung his hat. With the exception of the in-house politics and human drama, Cady expected that one was much the same as another.

As they were welcomed into the chief's office, Cady noted that his own chief had joined them. The captains were not there but Johnson and the FBI guy, with a couple of his friends, were in the office waiting. The chief welcomed them all, thanking them for coming on short notice, then reminded them that everything shared there stayed there. He reintroduced Johnson, but referred to the others only as from the National Security Administration.

That makes it official, Cady thought to himself. *We were right, something is going on, maybe something big and it doesn't just involve a couple of random shootings.*

"The mayor and the commissioner have already had this chat so they have elected not to participate in today's update," Jordan offered, answering the unasked question.

Johnson took the lead. "Our informant in Canada has given us credible intel that a well-funded and planned event is likely to occur within the next thirty days on American soil. Although it may involve several geographical locations, we believe they desire to make their initial statement here on the East Coast, likely in New York City. Evidence points to radical Muslim elements, possibly al Qaida or others holding anti-Christian views as the principal threat. We have yet to eliminate any of the three previously identified methods of attack but rather see them possibly working in concert to gain maximum effect."

"Slap the sleeping giant and run," Cady said under his breath, but loudly enough to turn heads and get nods of agreement. "We lost the war in Viet Nam because we couldn't identify the enemy, couldn't fight their war because of congressional constraints, because of public sentiment," Cady continued.

Johnson was aware of the sentiment that military held as to handcuffing them and expecting victory in spite of it. "Officer Miller, you are quite right, and I'm afraid it's not getting better. The American people hold onto a sense on invulnerability and cling to the notion that they can live any way they choose with God providing ultimate protection. They scoff at the idea that we are by our very nature more vulnerable than those nations who lack personal freedom."

One of the silent NSA men finally spoke. "Realistically you cannot have it both ways, unlimited freedom and security from the very people who claim the right to it. Sooner or later they will succeed in their efforts to show the world that our system of government is riddled with security problems. Forget for the moment suitcase bombs, sarin gas, ICBM missiles and car bombs, and picture a man in the forest with a single match and duplicate him a hundred times across our nation. How do you protect the nation from that?"

The room fell silent. They all knew he had just described the inevitable price of freedom, the same freedom Cain used to kill his brother, Abel.

"So," John said, "what do we do? Just quit trying?"

"Of course not," answered the NSA guy. "But we need to educate the public so they do not expect the impossible either. Grow them up a little. Help them understand that security is each person's responsibility not just law enforcement or the government."

Johnson took over again. "This should sound scary, because it is. Make no mistake, something will happen and likely soon. Our best efforts to prevent it will probably or already have delayed it. The commissioner, mayor, all of the chiefs and their subordinates will soon be holding vigilance training in an attempt to get even the beat cop to be looking at the threat through new eyes. The ACLU and other groups are expected to go crazy trying to protect the rights of the very people who pose the threat. For now the administration has given its permission to take off the kid gloves. Within reason we can profile, don't have to play nicey-nice during interrogations, and can take a little more liberties during searches when we feel justified. They are allowing us to err on the side of caution rather than waiting to become victims. I expect that the backlash will cause our window of opportunity to close quickly. Hopefully it will be enough to diffuse this crisis before it happens."

"Your ears only," he continued, "our team in Canada has outsourced the interrogation to a third party. They are using whatever means necessary to break the suspects and get the information that we so badly need regarding the planned use of the explosives found in their van. There is a typed, signed executive order in the President's drawer authorizing the use of extreme measures. However, it will probably never see the light of day."

Chief Jordan took the floor. "We are quickly and quietly hiring trained, able-bodied, ex- and retired police under the cover of private security. Using a newly organized security business that appears private but works directly under the commissioner, we are putting extra security in place in those locations most likely to be targeted. This is to minimize the public and the terrorists' perception of the increased security."

"You talkin' to me, Chief?" John said. "You givin' me my job back?"

Jordan laughed with the others. "John, you've always been on the job. We just took you off the payroll."

Again they laughed. It felt good to laugh again after the grim debate of the last two hours. Apparently, the NSA guests had been briefed on Cady and John's role in the mission because they readily accepted them as peers and comrades in the present battle against terrorism. It was 5:15 when they got to their car, and there was a ticket under the windshield wiper. Cady's blood pressure began to rise as he pulled it away and tore it open. "GOTCHA," was written across the face of the voided ticket.

They were still laughing as John dialed the cell and reached Helen on the third ring. "We're on our way," John said. "Where are you?"

"Resting our feet at 10421 Lamont Street. We bought so much we had to take a break and sit down," she answered.

John disconnected the phone. "10421 Lamont Street," he said. "They're waiting for us."

Cady began to laugh again. "Sure they are, John. Do you remember what is at 10421 Lamont?"

John missed the joke and for the life of him couldn't place the address until they pulled up in front of Baskin-Robbins.

The four friends were in a rare mood when they entered into traffic heading downtown toward Marshall's. Traffic was sluggish and congested, stop and go most of the way. They arrived only fifteen minutes before their seven o'clock reservations.

Out front of Marshall's Red paced back and forth nervous as a cat. When he saw the quartet approaching he gave them a broad smile.

"Was beginning to think you were joking," Red said to Cady. "I didn't eat all day so I could fill up on your tab."

They entered and were greeted, but before being seated, ADA Mitchell breezed in the front door behind them. Cady's mouth dropped. She looked stunning. Cady made introductions nearly laughing at Red who just stared, and was unable to find his voice. Her hair framed her face, with a hint of makeup giving her normally pale complexion more tone. Her freckles looking like angel kisses on her short nose. She had obviously 'dressed for the occasion,' not knowing who or what to expect of the others. Sarah looked like a queen, the others her court, and Red the jester. *Funny*, Cady thought, *I have never considered Sarah a woman but more of a colleague of indeterminate sex.* He had therefore never thought to try and pair her with his young rookie. It had just happened.

They were seated in a little private area quiet with subdued lighting in a back corner of the room. Light background music seemed to drift through the room the same way that the succulent aromas filled the air from the kitchen. The waiter brought a drink menu and suggested some $75 bottle of wine. Cady took a quick poll before buying two bottles of a house Cabernet for the same money.

Sarah seemed a little nervous when she broke the silence. "So, Shawna, you work with the free clinic?"

Shawna nodded, then answered, loving to talk about her passion. "Yes, but only three days a week. The other two I work with Health and Welfare."

Cady said proudly, "She has a nursing degree and a master's in social services," making it clear that she didn't just do filing.

"And family too?" Sarah continued. "When do you have the time?"

"I waited until our daughters were older before volunteering. I was a stay at home mom before we moved here."

"I envy you," Sarah said with obvious sincerity. "I have nothing but my career and few prospects."

Red had that "pick me, pick me" look on his face but said nothing.

"You mean a pretty woman like you doesn't have all those attorneys chasin' you?" Helen asked.

"I guess maybe," Sarah said, "if I had time to play their games. Most of them are married and just looking for a fling. Others want to get me into a compromising position where I can't do my job objectively. The "man pool" is full of sharks."

Everyone laughed.

When the waiter brought the wine the conversation slowed while they accepted their drinks and began to peruse their menus. He rattled off the chef's specials, his personal recommendations, then retired giving them time to make their choices.

What a diversity, Cady thought as he looked around his table of friends, *two Mics* (he guessed both redheads as Irish); *an American Indian; two cowboys; and an American woman, Helen.* He caught himself in his daydream feeling guilty for judging them by appearance.

Their food choices were just as varied: Shawna ordered leg 'o lamb; Sarah, fish; Helen, pasta; he and John, prime rib; while Red ordered stuffed pork chops. With their order finally taken, they all laughed again at their choices.

With the first bottle gone, the waiter served the second then appeared at their table followed by two other servers carrying their entrées. The food lived up to the restaurant's reputation. Each marveled at the flavor of their particular choice and traded bites so each could compare the dishes. In the end it was a satisfying and enjoyable time. They asked for coffee but held off on dessert temporarily as they addressed the reason for the meeting.

Sarah started. "Supervised probation two years. I was hoping to share that responsibility with John and Helen if they are willing. Counseling and public service seems to be Shawna's strong suit. Can you make a place for them to do public service at one of your two charities?"

Shawna nodded. "We love volunteers. How long?"

"The judge thought 500 hours each would keep them off the streets and out of trouble," Sarah answered. "That's about twenty hours a week for the two years of their probation. I think it is important to keep records so we all know what progress they're making."

Again Shawna nodded. "Done."

"Now," Sarah continued, "what's left for the guy who got us all into this, let me see." She was looking directly at Cady. Her voice took on a serious tone. "They need a father, a man's influence in their lives. Think the three of you men can handle that? Show them how a man lives, how he accepts responsibility, how he faces challenges and over comes them, how it is alright to be weak and sensitive when necessary, to show love and feelings, but to be strong and make tough decisions and stand by them."

This is quite a woman, was the shared thoughts going through the men's minds.

And I am not sure I am up to her standards, thought Red.

"Tomorrow is the last day of August. Is everyone on board? If so I'll tell the judge the clock is ticking."

Red was tempted to stick up his hand and ask for permission to speak, but did not. Felling a little out of place he quipped, "I was just here for the free meal. How did I get volunteered for this?"

Sarah smiled a smile at him that melted his heart. "Protect and serve, isn't that what you signed up for, Carrot Top? Well, it's time to serve."

Red had drowned in the pools of her eyes and would have died for her that instant, or married her without reservation. Trying to cover his shaky voice he replied, "Carrot Top? You are a good one to talk about red hair."

The room faded from their view. No one or nothing existed at that moment except Sarah and Red. For an instant it felt as it had felt when they had each accepted Jesus as their Savior, sharing a oneness, a sweet overpowering closeness, and love.

The other four watched them, enwrapped in one another for several seconds, then John broke the ice. "Dessert anyone?"

The waiter returned with the dessert cart and busily explained the various choices. Everything looked decadent, overdone, rich, fatty and delicious and was topped with syrups, sauces, nuts and whipped cream. In the end they only ordered three with each couple choosing to share their choice. It was nearly ten o'clock when they exited onto the sidewalk and began to say their goodbyes. Both Red and Sarah had arrived by cab and agreed to share one returning home. The Millers and the Days returned to the sedan.

The ride home was pleasant as they speculated on what the future might hold for Ted and Thomas, Sarah and Red, and for themselves. It was nearly midnight when they pulled into the driveway. A light had been left on in the kitchen for them. Their old white dog rose from his position on the porch and gave them a single woof before lying back down and going to sleep. Shawna had hinted at Cady to share the details of his meeting but dropped the matter when Cady was not forthcoming.

~

While entering church the following morning, Cady was pleased but very surprised to see Mrs. Brown with Ted and Thomas sitting with Red, John and Helen. Red had apparently extended the invitation as soon as he had gotten home last evening, which was gratefully accepted. Cady made a note to not underestimate his partner's convictions. The Millers had just seated themselves behind their friends and were making small talk when Sarah Mitchell entered as well. Red hurried to greet her and make room beside him for her.

"Cozy," Shawna whispered as she elbowed her husband and gave him a wink.

The music began with the choir taking its place on the podium while others continued to filter in. At the end of the second hymn the church was filled, with members being asked to move together to allow others to sit.

Pastor Orville took his place behind the pulpit when the music died out and said, "Welcome all to the Lord's house. I am pleased to see such a multitude this morning of both returning friends and new friends as well. I believe there must be something special that He has brought us together this morning to hear. Not my words, but His. Shall we pray and thank Him for His care over us?"

Orville lead them in fervent prayer as some followed along with him, others lifting up their own thoughts and words. Cady could hear murmurs, whispers, and almost the thoughts of others nearby him, but every time he closed his eyes he could see Sol's face once again. It would have been distracting except for the warm and friendly smile on Sol's young face. Ahead of them, Mrs. Brown and her sons were a little more vocal and charismatic than most in the room, coming from a background of a more open worship. Cady enjoyed seeing and hearing them and viewed it as a testimony to their faith.

Orville's message was on faith: its origin, growth and power. As with all good things faith originates with God. It is but a seed that we nourish by our acceptance of it.

"Each time faith overcomes, the victory gives us even greater faith. Doubt is always waiting to creep in and diminish our faith in its infancy." He quoted many profound verses, but few spoke to the actual mechanics of acquiring faith in the beginning. Orville continued that many who desire faith believe that they lack the knowledge of how to gain it. "Prayer, prayer is always the key. The key that opens the door to our understanding, to God's strength, and to growth in our faith as well. 'Ask and ye shall receive, knock and the door will be opened,' is oft quoted but not always understood," the pastor said.

As it turned out it was communion Sunday. Cady took note that the Brown family partook, indicating to most that they were believers and saved by Jesus' blood. The church held what is termed 'open communion' meaning that those professing faith are welcome to participate without qualifying with the church hierarchy in advance. Apparently some churches have a 'closed communion,' a qualification process, which is passing judgment as to who is worthy to take communion. Many in the crowd chose to remain after the service to enjoy conversation and a potluck in the downstairs meeting hall. The Millers, Days, Browns, along with Sarah and Red, were among those who remained. Cady hoped to gain Orville's ear for a few moments to discuss the ongoing presence of Sol in his life.

As they shared 'sup,' as John called it, they visited, discussing the sermon, their own personal spiritual walks, and their hopes for the future. Mrs. Brown, Bernice or Bernie as many referred to her, was open and very transparent in her beliefs, having been walking with God since childhood. She thanked them for their invitation and indicated that she hoped to make it a habit. The boys, welcomed by the Miller girls, had already made a few friends and met several from their school who were in attendance. Back in Idaho they might have been more of a novelty to the girls, but in New York there was a dominant ethnic culture, which made the girls almost the minority. Children are often less biased than their parents, seeing the person before making a big deal of the color.

Both Red and John visited with Ted and Thomas and were attempting to develop a friendship relationship with them while Shawna,

Helen and Sarah were quickly doing the same with Bernie. Orville left his table, having finished his meal, and was circulating among the remaining guests when Cady caught his attention.

"A minute with you pastor?" he asked.

"Of course," Orville said joining Cady at their table. "What's on your mind?"

Cady brought to mind the Bible study of the previous evening and particularly his encounter with Sol.

Orville smiled and asked, "Has he visited you again?"

"Well no, not exactly," Cady said, struggling to make his point. "But he has not left me altogether either. His face keeps appearing in my mind. I was hoping to get your opinion about that."

"Mr. Miller," Orville said, "you are a fortunate man indeed, and you give this old tired preacher too much credit. I have never been privileged to have had such an experience, although I would welcome one. Therefore, I can only speculate what may be happening to you spiritually. We can discount the presence of any evil force simply because of what he said and who he suggested you turn to for help, Jesus Christ. So, that leaves us with only two possibilities, that it was real or imagined. Because of who and what you are, because of your struggle to do good, your helping these two boys regain their lives, and your strongly held convictions, I vote for real. A secular shrink might disagree. As to why he seems to be 'hanging around' after delivering the message, I can only speculate that there is more to all of this than meets the eye."

Cady listened intently while the others grew quiet and were drawn into the pastor's evaluation. "Many times in Scripture, angels and even the Angel of God appeared to man to advise, protect and give counsel.

Although infrequent today, I speculate that it happens much more than is reported.

"Any thoughts on what unfinished business may be keeping Sol hanging around," Cady asked.

Orville answered, "You'd be a far better person to ask that question of yourself. What spiritual significance is going on that would justify God sending a special messenger to guide you through?"

Cady did not answer, but his mind went right to the investigation of the terrorists.

Orville continued, "Are there loose ends that need tied up that you have not completely addressed?"

John had been listening in and gave Cady a surprised look.

Sarah Mitchell handed out paper and pens around the table, having come equipped to continue where they had left off the previous night. Cady started to say, "Hey, no labor on the Sabbath," but kept quiet, knowing they were doing the Lord's work. Everyone was to write down their name, address, and phone number on each sheet. She then asked them to each commit to each other as her plan dictated: a meeting here, a phone call there, an activity, a labor, a friendly caring encouragement as conscience dictated. She also had some scheduled and necessary activities that the boys must attend. There were some questions asked but everything seemed well organized and straightforward. Sarah indicated they should meet together a minimum of once a month to evaluate how things were going.

The discussion was lively during the drive home, going off in several directions. It had been a busy and fruitful morning giving everyone much food for thought. At home there was a phone message from Ben in Florida. His message disappointed them all. He had to take a fill-in for another captain making it necessary to postpone their visit until the following week. They expected to arrive on Tuesday the 11th and were only able to stay a few days because of school.

~

On Monday morning Cady was back in the saddle, protecting and serving as it were, when his cell rang. It was John. He seemed delighted to be back at work, though in a limited and temporary capacity, working under the guise of security guard at the World Trade Center. From the public view he was a glorified doorman. In reality he had full written police authority from the mayor via the police commissioner.

"Get this," John bragged, "double my old salary and I only answer to Jordan or the commissioner."

"You been doin' some kissin' up have you?" Cady asked. "Any room for your old partner?"

"Afraid not, old buddy, they're only hiring the seasoned and disabled," he said with a laugh. "You are too young and not beat up enough yet."

Red continued to drive, without comment, overhearing only half of the conversation.

Cady volunteered what he could. "John's been hired, doing security, making a pile of money with no reports to fill out."

Red laughed. "Figures, some guys have all the luck."

"Seems like he may not be the only one. You and Sarah seem quite cozy for having just met."

Red turned red, or redder if possible. "We're just friends. We have agreed to take it slow and not mess up our friendship."

Cady grinned broadly. "Yep, that's what I thought. That's what Shawna and I said too."

Eight

Things were a mess. They had thought all their bases were covered, that the family could steal a little time and fly north for a few days. Nearly half of the school week had been blanked out with teachers doing in-service, whatever that was. The kids would only miss two days of school. Ben and his wife, Phil, were spending less and less family time and he was spending more and more time away from family. Living well certainly had its downside. Since the captaincy at United Airlines paid well, there were dozens of vets being discharged, just as Ben had been, and looking to get into the civilian side of flying. Especially enviable were those who were home based in the good locations like Florida, California or Hawaii. Ben's close friend had been a pilot on a return from Madrid when his copilot had to take the yoke. Acute appendicitis was the diagnosis when they touched down in Tampa. Subsequently emergency surgery affirmed that the appendix had burst leaving the likelihood of peritonitis a real threat. When the call came, Ben had tried to deflect the demand to postpone his plans, but was far from senior at the airlines. In the end he acquiesced to the pressure and called Phil with the bad news.

Between a rock and a hard place, a familiar saying to most, is not an enviable position in which to find oneself. United on one side demanding he perform, Phil and the kids playing the neglected family card on the other. Ben had inherited an overnighter, a flight to London then Paris, then a return the next day to Dulles International. He was to pickup a commuter there and arrive home on Wednesday where he'd be on standby through the weekend. When they called his mother, Kate, with the news of the change she begged off the chance to see Cady and family. She felt that they were close to a breakthrough in the search to unlock the mysteries of autoimmune disease. Her hope was to return to Africa someday with a vaccine to prevent or cure AIDS among the thousands stricken by the disease.

~

Guests were arriving at the Miller home by the carloads. Central to the event were the Brown family, Red and Sarah Mitchell. John and Helen were already helping Cady and Shawna with the grilling and food preparation. At the corral Faith and the twins had curried and saddled their horses for their guests as well as the young gelding that John had brought along. Each girl was eager to show her prowess as a horseman to Ted and Tom. Red and Sarah joined them and were enjoying the instruction of the young women. Bernie had brought a covered dish that she said dated back to her great-great-grandmother who had been a slave. Helen brought her own German potato salad.

When Cady looked, Faith was just dismounting from having given Sarah an instructional ride,. Sarah was left looking alone and uncertain in the saddle. On the other two horses, Ted and Tom were in the saddles with the twins on behind them. Red stood nearby with Faith smiling and shouting encouragement and last minute instructions.

"Ten minutes," Cady yelled toward the barn as the horses began to move. "We eat in ten minutes."

The twins were fearless, probably not the best choice of instructors for novice riders, but they were also caring and considerate, wanting the city kids to enjoy themselves. Always the worst choice was to want something more than a walk but less than a gallop, but that is just what a new rider always got. A nice trot, bouncing them up and down like Ping Pong balls in the saddle, fearing to go faster, but not wanting to slow to a disgracing walk.

Everyone was laughing hysterically when the dinner bell signaled time to eat, allowing the three new riders to dismount with dignity. Luckily, weather permitted outdoor dining because their high spirits could not have been contained in a building. An observer might have assumed they'd been friends all of their lives with the chiding and light humor spilling from their lips. Ravenous was the word that best described their appetites. Burgers and hotdogs, three dozen ears of corn, salads and steaming dishes soon disappeared as vapor on a mirror. Red and Sarah had stopped at Marie Calendars and bought three pies and a gallon of ice cream, none of which was left over. When the eat-a-thon finally finished, the adults sought out lawn chairs and coffee while the youngsters went back to the pasture, albeit more slowly to remount their steeds.

The early autumn sun had already set as the last of the cars pulled back onto the pavement and turned toward home. Cady helped Shawna in the kitchen while the girls put up the horses and stowed the tack. It had been an enjoyable and lighthearted day, one that made it hard to imagine that anywhere in the world lurked sadness and pain.

~

Later that night John called Cady. "Whatcha think of your new mount, brother?"

Cady wanted to laugh but did not. "A little scrawny seems to me. Did you buy him by the pound?" "You expect me to feed that thing so you can take it back and make money on it?"

John laughed. "I think it has Pony of America blood in it, and has not been properly fed or cared for. I doubt it will ever stand tall, but seems gentle and has a lot of heart."

"Like you," said Cady laughing. "Not too tall but with a lot of heart."

John only stood 5 feet 8 inches and carried his weight in his shoulders, hardly looking formidable when standing beside Cady. However, Cady quickly learned to respect his abilities and common sense approach to problems.

"Seriously, John, I appreciate it. It will give each of the girls one and save a lot of bickering as to who has to double up."

"The twins didn't mind doubling up behind the boys," John observed.

"Just being polite," Cady responded, slightly irritated by the implication.

~

The following morning after muster, as the teams broke out into pairs, the commander asked Cady and Red into his office.

"Word has trickled down to your lowly commander that they have broken one of the suspects in custody in Canada," he said. "It appears that the UN building was their primary target, working in concert with others who have also been arrested. These cells seem to know little of each other, just their part and a little about the overall game plan. I'm told that all law enforcement on the East Coast has been told to show special interest in foreign nationals or tourists from Muslim sympathizing countries. Two foreign exchange students from Sudan tried to claim their baggage in Grand Central Station and were found in possession of nearly a quarter of a million dollars in cash. They were unwilling to account for the money or prove ownership. The FBI has traced the money to a mosque in Canada with suspected terrorist sympathies and have little doubt it was to provide funding for weapons or explosives."

Cady felt cold chills and thought, *This is really happening, something big and bad.*

Cady and Red took a bogus 10-32, man with a gun call, from some prankster. They finished the morning out on a 10-7 at the coffee shop.

That Red had been allowed into the circle, was the commander's mistake, assuming probably that Cady shared everything with his partner. In any event, Red had been right on the edge of things all along and the error allowed Cady to be candid and forthcoming with him. It was easy now for Red to see why Cady and John had spent time with the chiefs and why their moods had reflected it. Red had no doubt been piecing it together himself following the taxi incident.

Cady's cell phone rang; it was John. Cady filled him in on the commander's update, expecting a response.

John remained silent for a long while before speaking. "I have been expecting it, but never thought I'd live to see the day. I wonder if we are living out the prophecies of Revelation."

Cady was thinking the same thing, but did not answer. "Well pal," Cady began trying to sound upbeat, "if that is the case we'll be leaving soon in the rapture. I wonder if there is a way to dig into it in Bible study tonight without sharing too much information?"

John sighed. "I may call Pastor Orville on my break and visit with him. America, like ancient Israel, has begun a downward spiral and continues to step farther and farther from God. Not heeding the lessons of the past is man's ongoing problem. We all find it hard to learn from others' mistakes."

Finally a call came from Cady's friend and former commander at the FBI, but he had little to add to what had been said by Chief Jordan. For just a moment Cady thought of suggesting that Shawna take the girls back to Idaho to visit their grandparents for a few days. The vision of Sol's face replaced it. *Our security lies in He who created it all, not in what we do or where we are*, Cady reminded himself. *Our destination is home and some will arrive before others at the home He has prepared for us.* As these thoughts flickered through his brain he became at peace once again. His fight for control was given up.

John honked, out of habit, and was already on his way to the door when Cady looked out the window. Funny how the horn blast had gone from a courtesy in the early years of automobiles, announcing one's intention to pass, to a warning or threat as society became angrier and more into themselves. John had simply announced his arrival. Shawna had just finished taking a couple dozen refrigerator cookies from the oven as the family, plus John, piled into the kitchen. Some grabbed milk, others lemonade, before settling down at the table to enjoy the treat. Uncle John made a mock play for the plate, causing giggles from the twins and a solemn look from Shawna. Finally someone blessed the food so they could argue over who deserved which one and how many.

On the drive into town John and Cady discussed the events of their day, with the senior man commenting on the impossibility of his job.

"There are fifty of us in each tower with thousands coming and going each day. Service personnel alone number in the hundreds with vendors and sales people calling on the individual businesses constantly. I have no idea how many regular security people are employed just to keep petty theft and arguments under control. Did you know that they have their own medical personnel on site?"

Cady shook his head, and said, "You can multiply that by a thousand if you consider other significant buildings and shopping centers just in the downtown area." *Yes*, he thought again, *security lies only in the Lord.*

No sign of his new Jewish friend, Sol, Cady noted as he entered the fellowship hall and joined the other men. There was a larger than normal turnout this evening, possibly as many as thirty, including several church elders who seldom came.

Orville opened in prayer and got right down to business. "We are going to wait until after our study before we take prayer requests tonight. We have a lot of ground to cover. First let me say nothing in God's Word stands alone. Everything is an integral part of everything else. That said, we are going to address passages out of Daniel and the Revelations of John, end of times prophecy. I have asked some of our elders to join us tonight so that we may break up into groups more conducive to discussion."

The men were looking at one another quizzically wondering where this all came from, moving from last week's theme of dependency upon God to end of times.

Orville must have read their minds, for he spoke again to the unasked question. "As we will see tonight, as the end nears mankind will find it necessary to draw closer and closer to God just to survive. I feel that part of God's plan is to force those who have remained distant, by depending upon their own resources, to humble themselves and accept salvation and Lordship."

"With those redeemed by Jesus absent from the earth, having been removed at the rapture, our world will be in turmoil," said Garth, one of the elders. "Many believe that the Holy Spirit will depart, giving Satan dominion over mankind for seven years before Jesus returns in victory."

Orville replied, "As with all prophecy there are many interpretations and opinions. We are going to offer you this church's consensus opinion while leaving you each the freedom to seek others."

A whiteboard had been added to the decor, allowing the pastor to illustrate and diagram as he spoke. "This is not meant as a theology lesson, or to convince anyone that our philosophy is the correct or true one," came Orville's disclaimer. "Let's focus first on the rapture, a word not found in the Holy Bible. Most Christian denominations believe that Jesus will remove the faithful from the earth at some point in time. I'll give you verses to record for your consideration that support this idea as I go along, but will not take time to discuss each in detail. The three schools of thought are: just preceding the final seven years leading to the end of times; at the mid-point, or three and a half years into it; and, after the seven-year period is complete. We, like many others, believe there is substantial doctrinal evidence that the first is the most likely. With that in mind, let's move forward assuming that to be true."

The four elders schooled up groups of about seven or eight with chairs facing each other. Orville remained standing at the white board and began to record some of the events he believed would happen and their order, with Scripture notations beside each. Spiral notebooks and pens were passed among the men present, who had obviously not come well prepared. Both John and Cady remained seated together, being shepherded by a youngish looking elder named Bart who Cady did not know. Bart was prematurely gray, but looked to be in his early forties, possibly a tradesman by his dress. He had a genuine smile and fiercely blue eyes.

Orville waited a few minutes for order to be restored then continued. "Since the early church, mankind has been waiting hopefully for Jesus' final return. The original disciples spoke as though it was imminent. Many expected it to happen during their lifetime. More than 2,000 years later we are still waiting and hoping for that day to come soon.

Many replied, "Amen."

"While many have tried to guess the timing, God's Word says that none shall know the hour or the day and that He will come like a thief in the night. But we are not left without warning. We are given clues to when that time is about to happen." Orville listed several passages on the board of things that must happen before the end of times.

Bart interrupted their thoughts saying, "We could easily spend a year studying this material in its detail."

Orville nodded agreement. "Many have spent their lifetimes trying to unlock God's secrets. There are events happening in our world right today that have encouraged me to try and help us gain at least a basic understanding of these Scriptures. It could happen next week, next year or in a hundred years, but someday soon. Those who have accepted Jesus as their Savior will be absent from this earth and with Him. That event is referred to as the rapture. Forget trying to understand or explain the mechanics of it or how it may happen, we will just be gone. Those not taken will be those who failed to embrace the free gift of salvation for whatever reason. Some will be friends or relatives, coworkers, and even faithful churchgoers, others are those who may have been mislead by false religions or have chosen to oppose God. The event of the rapture is believed to trigger the beginning of the seven-year period described in Scripture." Again he noted appropriate chapter and verse for their further research and study. "The events described will become worse and worse as time goes on. It will become harder and harder for those remaining to find salvation. An anti-Christ, empowered by Satan, will deceive the world and lead it farther and farther toward destruction and away from salvation. Few of those who come to faith after the rapture will survive to see Jesus' return, final victory, and His thousand-year reign."

The groups were in lively conversation, and some heated debate for the next hour.

Orville interrupted once again. "Brothers, none of us are likely to come to valid conclusions this evening given the complexity of the subject matter. What we have done is to open our eyes to a very real and certain future event. It should make each of us eager to witness – that none would be left behind."

Cady supposed each, like him, had just gotten a mental list of those to whom he felt drawn to witness. Cady remembered how John had explained the urgency he had felt to witness to him even before their knowledge of the terrorist plot became evident.

"Men," Orville said, "there are those for whom you personally may be the only witness enabled by God to open their eyes to salvation. I urge you to ignore your instinct to hold back, to be bold, and offer your witness to others."

Neither John nor Cady felt very conversational on the ride home, both feeling the weight of responsibility heavy on their shoulders.

The study had gone over its normal time, leaving Cady to arrive home near midnight. The old, white dog didn't even rise to greet him. He just opened one eye to see who encroached on the porch. Inside, a light in the kitchen welcomed him to the sleeping household.

Cady sat at the table with his head in his hands for several minutes before lifting up his voice in prayer. He first offered thanks for God's blessings, his family and friends, prayed for a new direction for his country, and finally prayed for those whom God loved that he knew only as enemies. When he opened his eyes they were wet with tears that blurred his vision, so he told himself when he saw Sol smiling at him across the table. Cady rubbed his eyes, but Sol remained.

"Sol is that you? Are you real?" Cady asked feeling foolish.

Sol nodded and spoke so quietly that Cady wondered if it was audible or if he had just sensed it. "Yes, it is me, and I am certainly real."

Cady felt reassured, then asked, "What are you? Are you an angel?"

Sol smiled broadly. "I am a messenger, sometimes called an angel. I am sent to watch over and guide you through your journey home."

Cady asked, "Why haven't I ever seen you before? Have you always been with me?"

"I have always been here with you. You have seen me many times but did not recognize me because you were not ready to believe," Sol answered.

"Are you my conscience?"

Sol laughed. "No, I am your guide and friend, but like any friend I try and help you make good decisions that will honor my Master."

"So why here, why now? Why did you appear, and why can I still see you?"

Sol laughed softly. "You give us too much credit. We don't know the future unless the Master tells us of it. We don't know the purpose for things unless He chooses to tell us. However, I have chosen to be visible to you that you may believe me when I attempt to guide you. Much the same as why Jesus chose to be born of woman and live as a man rather than a king. The Holy Spirit is strong, but sometimes a visual gives a better dimension of reality to the seeker of truth."

Cady was enjoying the exchange but wondered secretly if he may have dropped off to sleep and was dreaming the whole thing.

Sol must have been able to read his thoughts because he laughed again and asked, "Do you need me to speak louder or knock over the table or something to help you believe?"

Now it was Cady's turn to smile. "How about a cookie?" he said. He pushed the saucer with two cookies remaining toward his guest.

"I'd love one," came the reply. "We don't often get to eat worldly manna." He bowed his head asking for the Father's blessing on the food.

While Sol seemed to savor the cookie, Cady took the other, eating it without conversation.

"So," Cady said, "why can't others see you when I can?"

"They may or may not, but if they do they would likely see me differently than you do. I was with both you and Kate when your parents died. She was able to see me as I am, but you were not. More recently you saw me in the eyes of Bernie Brown when you offered her hope. I have often been there in the form of a vagrant to whom you gave a ride or bought breakfast. Sometimes I have helped you make the choice of using force or applying the bandage of love to your charges. I have no power to change events, just the ability to help you shape them."

"Do each of us have someone like you with us always?" Cady asked.

Sol considered the question before answering honestly. "I don't know." Then he laughed loudly and said, "The question has never come up around the water cooler."

Cady laughed too. Just the image of angels standing around a water cooler in heaven was more than he could take.

Sol seemed to be enjoying the conversation. "Are there more cookies?" he asked.

"I'm afraid not," Cady answered. "Perhaps a glass of milk?"

"Milk and honey," Sol mused. "Indeed this is the land of milk and honey. Do you have honey also?"

Cady rose and filled a glass with milk before taking a honey bear from the cupboard. He placed the glass before Sol and the honey bear with a spoon beside it. Sol raised the glass to his lips obviously savoring the cold, white liquid. Cady leaned across and squeezed a small amount of honey into the spoon while Sol watched.

Cady had a memory of Scripture. "Jonathan got in trouble for eating honey," he quipped. "Don't get yourself in trouble."

Sol looked right through him and said, "He got in trouble with the man Saul. I answer to God only."

Cady felt chastised. Apparently punishment from God is nothing about which to make sport.

Then he was gone. Just like that Sol had vanished. But the milk glass and spoon remained to testify of his visit. As Cady readied for bed, he picked up the glass and spoon and headed for the kitchen sink feeling a marvelous tingle in his fingertips. The clock by the bedside showed

12:05 as he slipped in beside Shawna. He mused that his entire conversation with Sol had only been a scant few minutes.

Morning arrived overcast and cold, threatening rain, the first of the fall season. Summer was officially gone, and soon the beautiful colors of fall would adorn the entire eastern seaboard. The green would remain of course among most of the conifers, the exception being the tamarack pines that turned bright yellow. The crimsons, reds, browns and yellows of the deciduous hard and softwoods would paint pictures in the mind to be long remembered. If one would but pay attention, the seasons told the story of mankind: of his birth, growth, decline, and finally death. But unlike the animals and plants, God chose that man, made in His image, would be eternal. Not eternal in our sinful world, but eternal in either heaven or hell by his own choosing.

After getting the girls off to school, Cady and Shawna rode in to the city together.

Cady finally broke to silence. "I saw an angel again last night," he said lightheartedly.

"Oh," Shawna answered, "and where was that? At Bible study?"

"No," Cady said, feeling apprehension at describing the unlikely event at the house, "in the kitchen."

"I see," said Shawna, "and was it your old friend Sol again?"

"Yes," Cady answered, "it was. We had milk and cookies together."

Shawna had been drinking from her coffee mug but now was rushing to wipe coffee off her clothes, the dashboard and windshield. Cady pulled over to the roadside and offered her his handkerchief while sporting a grin on his face.

After appraising the damage to her clothes she turned to him and said laughing, "You did that on purpose. You waited until I was drinking to give me the punch line."

Cady tried to look innocent without success. "We had a nice visit too. He likes honey with his milk."

Shawna raised an eyebrow. "What exactly were you drinking?"

"Nothing I swear," Cady laughed. "Sol called this the land of milk and honey and so I gave him both."

"And he ate and drank with you?"

"Yep, he said he didn't get the chance often to partake of our world."

"What else?" Shawna asked, sounding more serious now.

Cady thought, then replied, "He said he could not change events but could help us shape them. I took that to mean that we, by our free choice, have a certain amount of latitude to shape the here and now. But ultimately everything is under God's sovereign control."

"So," she said, "he can guide us and help us make good choices in an effort to glorify God in those choices?"

"Yes, maybe," Cady said. "It seems logical to me that God, in his plan for us, must maintain some control while still giving us free will to make mistakes."

"Sounds complicated to me, even for God."

"I agree. But of course knowing the final outcome of each life gives Him latitude to readjust His course to compensate for our errors." Cady thought for a moment then continued, "I have heard of a shipping company that has found it more expedient to make three right turns to get to a location rather than a single left. I see God sometimes letting us do likewise to arrive at the destination safely. Sometimes the shortest route is neither the quickest nor best."

Their conversation continued until she dropped Cady off at the station where he was working a staggered shift.

Red was waiting for him when he arrived, eager to hear how Bible study had gone. He had attended a few times but was irregular in his commitment, still struggling to totally disengage himself for the secular lifestyle of a young, single man. "How did it go?" he asked Cady.

"Well, the subject is deep and profound, frightening and yet for those of us saved, a blessing sure to happen. Most of us were overwhelmed by it, its enormity, finality, and then there seems to be no complete and uncontested interpretation of the events. Pastor Orville was quick to explain that his own beliefs, while widely shared, are also very possibly not totally correct and even possibly incorrect."

Red smiled. "If not the experts, who then can we believe?"

Cady shook his head. "Certainly not any man. Only God's Word, but in that we each lack understanding so we are forced to do our own legwork and ask God for His help."

"Seems to me that it is more likely to happen while we are still trying to figure it all out."

"Could be," Cady agreed. "Men have been struggling to unravel God's mysteries from the beginning. And, I wonder if we have learned anything at all, if we are any closer today than when Jesus walked among us. I can give you a copy of the Scripture references from last night to research but suggest you try and make it next week for the study."

"I'd like that," Red said. "Maybe Sarah and I can discuss it together during the week. She's pretty sharp on the Bible."

Cady smiled but said nothing about them becoming an item so quickly.

At lunchtime Cady and Red were 10-7 at the free clinic where Shawna worked. Unfortunately she was in counseling with a young woman and could not be disturbed, so they had a quick lunch nearby. As their day wore on, the weirdos came out of the woodwork, fictitious calls, bad addresses, combative shopkeepers and customers, the whole gamut of society. The blessing was nothing serious or life threatening happened on their watch.

While waiting for Shawna to pick him up, Cady began to think about the events that had been described at Bible study. Many seemed to be already happening in our world: natural disasters, wars, idolatry, persecution, inhumanity. The list went on and on. *All we need now is the anti-Christ and false prophet,* he mused. *I wonder if we will recognize them when they appear. A wolf in sheep's clothing,* he thought. *Was that Hitler, Mao, Saddam or someone yet to come? Was the holocaust one of the events prophesied and some still future one the trigger?* He felt himself being sucked back into insecurity and uncertainty for lack of understanding. He prayed. His prayers were not immediately answered but interrupted by a horn blast from Shawna's car.

A quick call home verified that all the little chickens were safely in the hen house waiting eagerly to be fed. Cady disliked the ten to six shift but suffered with it every twelve weeks, as did everyone else on patrol, in an attempt to provide round-the-clock protection. They tried to ride together the days their shifts meshed. The other days they took separate cars. At 7:15 they arrived home with a double crust, double-stuffed cheese pizza topped with everyone's favorites. Fifteen minutes later the feeding frenzy slowed as they eyed the scant remains trying to decide if they had room for another piece.

With their homework already done and dinner out of the way, the girls were eager to share the events of their day. It was a time of tragedies, dramas, successes and disappointments – the school day – when seen through they eyes of a young woman. Both Cady and Shawna loved to listen to the young voices trying hard to make their listeners imagine the magnitude of each victory or defeat by the passion in their delivery. Overall, few evenings failed to end in laughter.

Cady invited Shawna to go for a horseback ride, something they rarely did, as the shadows of night were fast falling. Together they rode down their lane then along a graveled frontage road lined with trees, neither one feeling the need to speak. It was as if they had turned back the clock a dozen years and more, still living in Idaho. *Crickets must live everywhere*, Cady thought as he heard their choir sing the familiar songs. Overhead the moon was appearing intermittently between thin gray clouds as darkness overtook them.

Suddenly Shawna pulled her horse up short, stopping. Cady did likewise, turning in alarm to find the reason.

"I wonder," she said, "if a thousand years ago, a man and a wife such as us rode this same land under these same stars. And if they shared hopes and dreams for their family and of the future, without fear."

Cady could not find words to answer, but knew none were expected. They kissed deeply, leaning toward each other, with horses reigned close together. The old spark of remembered passion flickered into a flame that left them feeling young and foolish.

Cady finally spoke, his voice still husky. "Maybe it is time to head home."

"Maybe," she answered.

They awoke early still in each other's arms welcoming the rising sun to Tuesday morning, September 4. He had two more days of the ten o'clock shift before moving to the noon to eight shift. The girls were arguing over the bathroom, and the white dog was sleeping at the foot of the bed. Shawna, ten years his junior, was playing with the hair on his chest. Most full-blooded Indian men had little body hair, so when they had met, she had been intrigued by his beard, leg, and chest hair. He smiled. There was still a little girl in her that shone through occasionally. On his way to their bathroom, he went to the kitchen and started the coffeemaker. Shawna joined him in the bathroom and brushed her teeth while he showered. He shaved, dressed and joined the family in the kitchen just as bacon, fried eggs and hot cakes hit the table.

Sometimes Cady wondered how he survived the mood swings of four women. Two of the girls weren't hungry, one was ravenous, and the other could eat. He knew they were all hungry but eager to be forced into it. They prayed thanking God for the day, His provision for them, and for His protection over them. Cady served two cakes, one egg and two strips of bacon to each, watching them roll their eyes. It was a family ritual as though he was forcing them to fatten for the slaughter. Each girl so very conscious of her figure now, both Shawna and Cady worried about them adopting eating disorders. In the end, each ate every bite without urging then fought for the last strip of bacon on the plate before heading to school.

Shawna brushed her long, black hair before dressing then joined Cady in the kitchen where he had just finished putting the dishes in the dishwasher. Dog, so named to make things simple, had taken the final three cakes in a single bite and with soulful eyes scanned the kitchen for more. Cady filled both the food and water dishes before meeting Shawna at the car. The horses still had good pasture and water from the stream that cut across their ground. Later in the year he would need to give them both water and hay each morning.

They discussed the young Puerto Rican girl Shawna was counseling and the progress she was making in accepting the baby as a gift rather than a curse. Health services had met with her and had a potential pair of adoptive parents of Caribbean heritage willing to take the child. Emotionally the last trimester was a roller coaster for young girls. Only time would tell what her final decision might be, which was still months from now. Shawna prayed with her and for her often, wondering if the effect of introducing her to their family might be positive or negative. She decided to wait until late term and then discuss it with the family before doing so. Shawna had planned to leave work at four o'clock then spend a couple of hours at the free medical clinic before picking Cady up after his shift.

Nine

The slasher, what the watch commander had named him, made several assaults on ethnic women where he replaced their veils with knife wounds. This happened in the last twenty-four hours. Young, male, dark hair and eyes, slim build, twenty to thirty years old was the reoccurring description. The targets had all been young, single, and Middle Eastern women who had abandoned traditional dress for American apparel. None seriously injured, but all permanently disfigured was the medical report. Hissim was the squad's only expert on the growing Middle Eastern segment of the borough. When he spoke he tried to impart the serious tone of the attacks. They would escalate to murder if left unchecked. In their homeland death was the sentence for breaking the customs, with women having no rights at all. Often a member of the woman's own family would kill to restore the family honor.

As they began patrol, Red and Cady discussed the case and wondered how law enforcement could ever stop the attacks. It came down to looking for the potential victims rather than the assailant, then maintaining surveillance on them.

Cady made a call to the bookends, catching Barnes at his desk. "Cady here, had a thought about the slasher. Wondered if you had considered the use of a decoy to draw him out."

"Good thought. That same point was brought out in our briefing this morning. The team handling it is looking to find a couple of undercovers willing to give it a try. Turns out we don't have a lot of willing female officers who fit the description. We don't graduate a lot of Muslim women from the academy."

"Hear you there," Cady agreed. "Most aren't career oriented for the same reason they are being persecuted. How about calling it a hate crime and maybe getting help from the feds? Big brother may have a deeper resource pool."

"That's a thought," Barnes agreed. "I'll run it by the boss. Thanks for the input. Oh, by the way, we may have caught a break in the shooting on the pier. It appears the boat theft may have been just a cover. After a lot of digging, we found the boat registered to a holding company that is a subsidiary of an organization that holds a tax deferred status, The Center For Islamic Cultural Studies, based in D.C. When the feds checked fingerprints against visas and passports in the organization your warehouse caller showed up as an employee along with the deceased shooter. Both had been in the states less than six months. My bet is the two burned up in the taxi bomb incident were also, though we lack DNA evidence to compare with."

Cady listened trying to absorb, catalog and evaluate this new information. "Thanks for keeping us in the loop. I'll let John know."

He felt compelled to copy-in Red as well.

When he did, Red came back with a novel idea. "Seems like the feds should require a DNA sample before granting entrance into the country for use should any future identification become necessary."

Cady laughed. "Never happen, the ACLU would find it against a terrorist's rights to be forced to give evidence used later to arrest them."

John listened to Cady without interruption then said, "I'd like to call Chief Jordan, see if he is up to speed and if there is anything more that we don't know."

Cady nodded.

John continued, "What would you say to a get-together with Hissim and our one and only Christian convert in the church for a little brain storming session, off the record?"

"Why off the record?" Cady said. "I like the idea, a lot. See what the Chief has to say about it when you talk with him."

What had changed in the past few months? Cady was asking himself. *First, America's enemies were becoming more aggressive and more visible; second, less clandestine and more overt, seemingly without fear of retribution.* He had no depth of understanding of their culture, only knowing the little he had read in newspapers and magazines. He did know, however, an enemy, any enemy who had no fear of death was dangerous. To deal with one who saw death as a reward was impossible using normal tactics. *So,* he thought, *what is it that they do fear, if not death? Only that is the weapon that will even the playing field.* He made a mental note to ask Hissim should they have opportunity to meet.

They were 10-7, having lunch, at the bistro when the call came. John had contacted the chief who had OK'd the meeting with the stipulation that they report the results directly back to him. He had also called Orville and ran the plan by him as well. Orville was less enthusiastic about their plan to use a brother's race to gather intel to use against his countrymen. In the end, however, he agreed, remembering the many times spies and deception were used in the Old Testament times for God's own purpose. John had promised to pray into it, to seek God's direction, and follow His leading in the matter. Cady agreed to speak to Hissim then set up a meet, if possible, at their earliest convenience. A three-vehicle pileup in a busy intersection and the reports following finished up their day. Apparently a delivery truck had tried to make it through on a yellow/red only to be T-boned by two taxis who were eager to jump out on the green without looking first. Dispatch sent a second unit to provide traffic control and two wreckers who left with the two cabs. The intersection finally cleared as the truck drove away on its own power.

Shawna arrived a few minutes early and Cady remained a few minutes late, causing her to spend time visiting with the desk sergeant. Dan had always been a favorite of hers, an Irishman with a round body and lively sense of humor, overdue for retirement. They bantered back and forth arguing over any subject, always choosing opposite stances, before inevitably agreeing in the end. When Cady approached them they became immediately quiet as two children caught in some act, sharing a wink between them.

"So," Dan said, "you trying to get in a little overtime are ye, or kissin' up to the commander lookin' for a raise? Your little miss here has been waitin' most part of an hour for ye."

Cady smiled answering, "Why thank ye, Mic. You're always the happy one to keep an eye on the lassies aren't ye?" Cady knew his Irish dialogue was bad, making it all the more effective.

On their drive home they took turns letting off steam, asking questions without expecting answers or solutions. Cady was dying inside to share the information about what he was beginning to call the Islamic Conspiracy, to get her insight and opinions, but knew he could not. If he slipped, as had the watch commander, the circle would broaden, and another would slip, and another innocently would share with a friend. Ultimately it would leak to the press and they'd lose any chance to catch or stop the enemy.

~

The slow cooker had done its job. As they walked toward the house they could smell the aroma of roast beef. Dog, a Great Pyrenees, came to attention as they passed, wanting no doubt his share of the meal. To their delight they found the table set, drinks poured, and three beautiful girls smiling at their accomplishments. The cares of the day were swept away in an instant as they washed up and were seated at the table. Cady blessed the food, thanking God for His provision and asking for protection and forgiveness for them all. Smoke came from the oven causing the alarm to squeal and Faith to jump from her chair. The surprise had been meant to be Rhoades frozen bread rolls, but turned out to be little burned hockey pucks. They laughed at the faux pas while Shawna pointed out the need for them to defrost and raise before being baked. Outside they were black and inside they were still frozen.

The event was filed away in their memories for all time under family humorous events, waiting until some future date to be used in conversation. Faith knew she'd have the opportunity to laugh about it with her own children someday. The light tone set, they cleared the table together and rummaged through their selection of board games. They then spent the evening trying to best one another. At nine o'clock they took a break giving Cady the opportunity to touch base with John by phone.

"Shawna's off early tomorrow. Maybe I'll take my car in too. That way Hissim and I can meet you after I get off. That sound good?"

"Yeah, fine," John answered. "I'll call him. Where do you want to meet?"

Somewhere quiet where we can talk but not draw attention," said Cady.

"How about that little coffeehouse on West 139th? Joe to Go or something I think. They have little private cubicles where people meet to visit, read or do business."

"It's a date then. We'll meet you there a little after six o'clock." Cady turned to find Shawna looking at him. "That was John," he offered lamely. "We are going to meet right after I get off tomorrow for a few minutes. I figured it might be easier if I drive myself in so you don't have to wait around."

Shawna knew that the meeting did not include her and that the subject matter was off limits for some reason. She was plainly irritated but tried hard not to show it. "Fine," she said, turning away.

Not fine, Cady thought. *Not fine at all*. They had always had an open marriage, able to discuss anything, finding a way through it with God's help. Now here he was keeping secrets and hurting her by doing so. Cady had no clue where to go from here, so he wisely went to God. He bowed his head asking for God's direction and a softening of Shawna's heart. By the time he finished, Shawna had cleared up the game and the girls had gone to their rooms to prepare for bed.

He sat at the kitchen table with a glass of milk watching her move about the small kitchen, loving her until it hurt. He called her name softly, which she ignored at first, then again with some urgency.

When she turned her dark eyes were rimmed with tears. "I'm sorry," she said.

"No," answered Cady, "I'm sorry. Sorry for being unable to share with you certain things as I have always been able. There are things going on now that I am sworn to keep private, even from you because of their potential danger. A burden a few of us share together for a while yet."

She softened. "Does it have anything to do with the shooting?"

Cady only nodded, not wanting to be drawn into conversation.

"Then, that is why it includes John?" she continued.

Again he nodded.

"Are the girls in danger?" she asked finally.

Cady thought then said, "We are all in God's hands. Nothing that happens, happens without His permission."

Cady could see alarm in her eyes, fear, and for the first time he wished he had sent them west. He took her hand and remember the song lyrics, *Trust and obey, for there's no other way ...* "Please just trust me, and if not me, trust Him."

While trying to comfort her he knew the more he said the more the alarm bells were going off in her head. He bowed his head once again and prayed for God's comfort for her.

He went to bed but couldn't sleep. His mind was running full out searching for answers where there were none. Scenarios, one after another playing over and over like old movies. Check and checkmate, were the last thoughts he had before drifting off sometime after four o'clock.

Shawna had already showered and dressed, fed the girls and sent them off to school when Cady entered the kitchen. He found his coffee waiting but cold.

He started to speak, but she cut him off, "Let me warm that up for you. You needed your sleep so I didn't wake you."

"Thanks," Cady answered sheepishly. "I had a miserable night. It was almost morning before I drifted off."

She took his hand, looked him in the eyes and softly said, "You're just a man, Cady. A good man, but still flesh and bones. Be careful for me, for us."

"I will," he promised. "I always do."

Shawna kissed him with meaning and headed out to her car.

Ten

Cady took a few minutes to check the horses and that Dog had been fed before leaving for work. On the drive in, he turned off the radio choosing rather to pray aloud. He emptied himself to the point of weakness as he stood naked before His Lord. Seldom had he felt so out of control but so close to Jesus.

He checked in, stood roll call, got updates on the events of the ongoing investigations, then started to join Red in the car when Hissim caught his arm.

"Six o'clock then?" Hissim asked. "I meet you here?"

"Yes," Cady answered, feeling the apprehension return. "Then we'll meet them at the coffee shop on 139th."

Turning toward the door again, Cady was stopped by Barnes. "Your perp, the warehouse guy that you shot up, died last night. The medical examiner thinks it might be a homicide. Someone got to him with our guy right outside of his room."

"He'd never have talked," Cady stated.

"Yes, you are right," Barnes agreed. "But I don't think they wanted to take the chance. Someone must have found out that we had connected him to the CFICS in D.C. and wanted to prevent further fall out."

"Thanks for the update," Cady threw over his shoulder. "I appreciate it."

Finally making it to the car where Red was waiting, Cady said, "Sorry partner, got a late start this morning then got stopped twice leaving the building."

Red smiled. "You look bad too," he chided. "Rough night?"

"Couldn't sleep, kept playing this thing over and over in my head," Cady answered. "Barnes just told me our towelhead from the warehouse was murdered last night in the hospital."

"Wasn't he under guard?" Red asked.

"Yeah, for all the good it did. Probably someone dressed like an orderly went in and gave him a needle," said Cady in disgust.

"Man, the plot thickens!"

"That it does, friend, that it does," Cady agreed.

At 10:47 they were called 10-18 to a clothing store where a suspect was being held by a security guard for shoplifting. Caught on camera it was a slam dunk. They took her to booking then returned to the street. By that time they had missed their daily 10-7 at their favorite coffee shop so Cady chose to drive by the one on 139th instead. They parked and checked in 10-35 at the location then entered to get the lay of the land. It was easy to see why John had chosen it. It had several booths in the rear faced out, giving them clear view of anyone entering or leaving. Officers often sought out such an arrangement that they may keep their policeman's eyes on the crowd.

A little highbrow for their usual tastes, nevertheless they both ordered foo-foo coffee, which they drank in their car. The shift started at ten o'clock, which gave them a late lunch hour, and both were ready when two o'clock came. They stopped at a little Italian grinder near the middle school and had meatball subs, laughing at the number of napkins it took to keep their blues clean. When they returned to their car they saw two familiar faces walking toward them with big smiles, Bill and Joe. The pugilists looked pleased to see them again, and walked right up.

Cady smiled. "Boys, nice to see you again."

"We were hoping to see you sometime," Joe said. "Me and Bill wanted to apologize to you for the way we acted and thank you for the ice cream."

Red smiled at them and asked, "So men, which one of you got Mary Ellen?"

"Neither of us," Bill said. "We decided being friends was more important than women."

"Yeah," Joe added, "women are trouble."

Both Cady and Red smiled then Cady said, "Remember that Red."

"Officer Miller," Bill started, "we wanted you to know that we both have decided to be policemen someday like you."

"That's nice to know boys. I take that as a real compliment. It gives me something to live up to."

Red laughed. "How about me?"

"Yeah you too," Joe added.

"Well, keep the grades up. NYPD requires college now too, so you need to work hard and keep your noses clean. Stay out of trouble." "You need anything, call us," Red said handing them his card.

Red got behind the wheel, Cady shotgun.

"Cool!" Red said. "That was almost like leading someone to Jesus. I wonder what it would be like to see that pair in 20 years?"

"They'd look just like you, partner, only without the red hair and big ears," laughed Cady.

They entered traffic notifying the house they were available.

"What do you mean big ears? Sarah likes them," Red said.

"I'm sure she does. They kind of grow on you, I hardly notice them anymore."

At six o'clock Cady walked into the coffee shop where three men were seated waiting for him. John had already introduced Hissim to Ukiam, the church's only Muslim convert, by the time Cady joined them. Cady took the lead, attempting to lay out the reason for the meeting without sharing too much of what they already knew. Cady mused at how it very nearly resembled using a former member of the drug culture to gain information about the current movers and shakers in the trade. Although not currently on the inside, they seemed to have the ear to the ground picking up bits and pieces that would be foreign to an outsider. Ukiam seemed eager to establish himself as a Christian who had chosen Jesus over Mohammed, but still reluctant to be totally forthcoming in matters that he regarded as politics. In his homeland they were one in the same, but here they were purposely held separate making it difficult to understand his new position.

Taking a new approach, Cady spoke to him. Speaking not of ideologies but rather of good and evil, right versus wrong, Cady emphasized that God loved all of His children equally but judged right from wrong by His own standards. No one had the right to take a life just because he disagreed with him, as the radical Muslims claimed to have the right. Ukiam finally gave them two names who had been known to support the radical movement, cautioning them he had no firsthand knowledge of their involvement. Regarding the slasher, Ukiam concurred with Hissim's assessment that he was most certainly a Muslim who felt that women who abandoned the traditional cultural dress and decorum shamed and dishonored their families. It was the equivalent of the 'scarlet letter' branding of early America. He suggested that certain clothing districts catered to the Americanized, free thinking, young Muslim women who desired to dress mainstream. Cady reported back to his commander and to Chief Jordan, leaving the follow up to the detectives, but suggesting that placing a very visible decoy in the clothing district may produce fruit.

Cady was working the noon to six on Thursday when he took a call on his cell. John and his cronies had intercepted two suspects who had attempted to enter the building in the early morning rush. The metal detector had picked up something, and the subsequent pat down had evidenced concealed weapons on each man and containers of liquids believed to be corrosives or chemicals to be used in concert with others to make lethal gas or explosives. The FBI had the suspects in custody with their lab working to identify the liquid. It was the first real hard evidence since the taxicab incident. Cady thanked him then called Johnson at Quantico. Johnson shared that a strip search had found the suspects' clothing yielded high levels of cyanide infused into the fabric that could be easily released into the atmosphere by soaking them in water. Nothing yet on the clear liquid. Both were in complete isolation being questioned but without success. Security at all federal buildings and others identified as probable targets had been increased.

While it appeared that the media had not gotten the scent yet, the first responders, their families, and close friends had no doubt noted that something was afoot. Coast Guard, customs, transit authority, border patrol, immigration, national guard, as well as firefighters and the thin blue line were working long hours, making it impossible to keep the alert undercover. When the mayor gave an executive order on Friday to curtail small sightseeing aircraft flights over the city, it finally made the news with several tourists complaining loudly. The backlash forced the mayor's office to issue a statement that they had received threats that must be taken seriously, while minimizing them in the same breath.

Chief Jordan invited Cady and John to a top-level meeting on Saturday, September 8, at the mayor's office asking them to listen but not offer advice unless asked. The feds were well represented with FBI, NSA and CIA present as well as military and FEMA. The mayor, commissioner, and heads of all city services were present. To his credit, the mayor kept a cool head, put away the pomp of the office, and became a colleague to his subordinates, giving up the mic to those better suited. When Cady recognized the deputy secretary of defense he became alarmed. Just to have him in the room gave the proceedings gravity beyond comprehension. Cady wondered if there might be a nuclear threat not previously considered until now.

The Canadian connection had yielded a minimum of detail, but confirmed the intent and commitment. That their own man had been assassinated while under police guard in the hospital added weight to the concern. The FBI lab confirmed the clear liquid captured at the towers to be corrosive acid, possibly to be used to disable elevators, fire control equipment, or fresh air systems. The cyanide added a note of seriousness and further commitment to the suspect's plan. Over a dozen suspected possible insurgents had been stopped and were being detained and questioned across the eastern seaboard. Sites harboring explosives in the coal mining regions were under increased security round-the-clock. Cady knew instinctively all this activity had been expected and considered by the terrorists, but what he wondered was their plan to counteract it.

Sol had joined him, sitting in a vacant seat to his left. Cady was tempted to ask John if he had seen him, but did not. Rather he gazed at Sol quizzically. Sol sent him a "mind message" before he disappeared: *Your security lies in the Lord.*

Solemn faces spoke of probabilities, of responses, of casualty counts, and of worst and best case scenarios. No one in the room continued to speak of prevention anymore. The reality of the situation had finally struck each individual, although none acknowledged it. Mankind had invented means to eliminate itself, and madmen had the conviction to use them against each other. Albeit depressing, the vision of Sol's face and his message diminished the gravity of the situation for Cady. When the meeting broke up he was resolved but not languishing in despair. Cady and Red finished their shift without incident and without a great deal of conversation.

~

Cady finally arrived home after nine o'clock. The girls had already eaten but waited to share the trials and victories of their respective days before going to their rooms to finish homework. Shawna looked tired and for the first time in memory, her age. Cady made note to stop at the florist on his way home tomorrow. He carefully approached the forbidden subject, not completely sure if he should share or spare her from worry. He knew that she was astute enough to know too much already. That alone caused her to worry but did not give her a cause.

He waited until they were in bed then gathered her up in his arms and said, "No one, I mean no one, including our own family, can be told what I am going to share with you." He felt her shiver in his arms. "The federal agencies have been monitoring a terrorist threat for several years now. Until lately indicators have not been alarming. But more recently there has been substantial evidence that the threat is both real and imminent. John and I were drawn into it by the shooting incident on the pier. It was our first hint that something was going on. Since then we have been included with groups and agencies that have been investigating and working to prevent an attack. There seems to be more and more evidence that the East Coast is the target area, with New York City having many potential specific targets."

Shawna was putting it all together in her head very rapidly, event after event now making sense to her. She did not speak, deferring to her husband who continued to explain how he had personally been involved in several situations. When he finally stopped speaking he was both exhausted and relieved to have finally shared his burden with her. Her questions were direct and concise: how, when, where, what and who? Most of them he could not answer with certainty, just generalities and best guesses.

"Do you think we should keep the girls home from school? Will we be safe here at home? Could it be nuclear? How soon do they expect it? Can they be stopped?"

To the last he replied, "No, I don't think so, not by man. There are too many weaknesses in our defenses to prevent a madman from doing something insane to others. My FBI friend said it best, 'Our freedoms give our enemies freedom to work against us.'" He hesitated before continuing, "Sol was with me for a minute in the meeting today and gave me a message. 'Our security lies in the Lord,' he told me."

With that they turned to God in prayer, tears running down their cheeks as emotion overcame them.

They awoke to early morning sunshine in their faces, the sounds of activity in other rooms of the house, and an urgency to attend church.

Faith, looking like a younger version of her mother, stood with a spatula in hand directing traffic in the kitchen. The twins, her lackeys, grumbled but moved swiftly setting the table and preparing for breakfast. Obvious that she was eager to redeem herself for the incident with the frozen rolls, she had French toast and bacon sizzling on the stovetop. Hope was filling glasses with orange juice, and Charity was filling mugs of hot coffee when their parents entered the kitchen. Cady was overwhelmed with emotion at his blessings and with fear at not having the ability to protect them from harm. When he looked at Shawna, she mirrored what he was feeling. Under her smile was pain and worry difficult to mask. When Faith blessed the food with a smile, the lump in Cady's throat threatened to choke him.

Dog waited patiently. His attention focused on each bite that passed their lips, getting only an occasional scrap of fat. The girls scampered to their rooms to dress leaving Cady to police the kitchen while Shawna showered. He took the rest of the egg batter poured it over the final three slices of bread and fried them up for Dog who smiled at him across the room. When the phone rang, Cady grabbed it expecting the worst. Rather it was the happy voice of his nephew, Ben.

"Hi Unc, just wanted to make sure we have a place to stay and free food next week. We should be in early Tuesday, but Mom can't make it this trip."

Cady assured him that there was always room and also how the girls had been counting the days until they arrived. "I work noon to eight Monday and Tuesday but have taken the rest of the week off to catch up with you."

~

They arrived just as the first hymn finished, looking hard before finding room for five to sit together. Cady remarked that attendance was up since school had been in session and most had finished their vacations. It had always irritated Cady when some took a vacation from God, saying that they needed time for themselves. The inference was that worship to them was a duty and not a privilege. He knew one of his greatest weaknesses was his judgmental spirit but chose to acknowledge it rather than abandon it. Orville's sermon seemed to lack the punch that Cady looked for every Sunday, something to lock away in his heart and carry with him throughout the week ahead. It was not until Orville quoted Jeremiah chapter 49 verse16 that Cady took note, applying it to his life and current situation. As he raised his head from the Scripture, a smiling face greeted him. Sol was standing elbow to elbow with Orville at the front of the room.

He elbowed Shawna and said, "There he is standing right next to Orville. Can you see him?

"Of course," she said, "that's Brother Garth."

When Cady looked again, it was Garth and not Sol who smiled back at him. *Am I going crazy?* he asked himself, unsure of what he had seen.

The service ended at 10:30 but the girls wanted to spend time with their friends, so they all went to Sunday school. Cady chose an open seat beside Hissim and his wife, taking time to introduce Shawna to them. He noted that she dressed as was customary in her homeland, making him wonder if she was a believer.

Unsurprisingly the empty seat customarily left at the table was occupied by Sol this morning. The lesson was about Biblical cities with a modern day video showing many of those that still remain and artists' depictions of others gone long ago. Cady had previously paid little attention to the terms "walled cities" or "fortified cities" when he studied the Bible, but now he found it interesting at how many references there were in Scripture. From early times mankind put his trust in things he could see and touch, finding comfort in creating barriers to protect themselves from their enemies. In Genesis there was mention of a gate allowing or preventing entrance into the Garden of Eden. Throughout Scripture were mentions of gatekeepers, walls, and fortifications behind which God's children took refuge. Cady's mind turned to New York City comparing it with Tyre, the great city by the sea. Not much had changed except the methods used to dissuade enemy attack.

All at once he knew what Sol had meant – any security is no security unless it depends upon God's power. Perhaps America might learn the lesson when the time came that others had failed to learn. Cady closed his eyes and prayed. He prayed for God's mercy and for open eyes and ears for His people. When he lifted his head, Shawna was watching him while Sol nodded his agreement. They had not been able to visit with John and Helen before or during the service because of their tardiness, but they took time to do so after Sunday school. Bernice and her sons were there as were Red and Sarah, walking arm in arm as they approached.

Sunday afternoon was gone by the time they finished their fish and chips lunch on the pier and drove home.

Shawna asked the girls to make sure their laundry was done and the house ready for guests on Tuesday before they ran off to ride the horses. She and Cady then joined Dog on the front porch where they failed to discuss what was foremost on their minds. They chose rather to discuss the sermon and the pending sunset. Cady couldn't avoid sharing his revelation regarding walled cities to which Shawna smiled and nodded.

Apparently she had already come to the same conclusion as he, only somewhat sooner.

Monday arrived with a stiff autumn breeze and threatening clouds overhead. The weather wizards had said little chance of rain on the late news, but Cady threw in his duty coat just in case they were wrong then prepared to leave for the city about ten o'clock. Shawna, who had taken the week off to prepare for and entertain their guests, kissed him goodbye before re-entering the house to get out of the wind. Cady was smiling while listening to David Jeremiah on the radio and enjoying the drive when Sol joined him in the passengers seat.

"Good morning," Cady said pleasantly.

"Yes, it is," answered his golden-haired guest. "Another of the Master's great works.

"Indeed that is true," Cady agreed as he noted the majesty of the billowing clouds blowing in from the Atlantic. They rode in silence for several minutes. "So old friend, is this a business or personal visit today?"

Sol looked puzzled, apparently unfamiliar with the difference between the two. Finally he smiled and said, "I am always personally about the Master's business."

Cady laughed openly. "Good answer, my friend, as we should all be."

"You seem less burdened today," observed Sol.

Cady smiled. "I suppose I am," he agreed although not having really considered it. "Is burdened one of those Christian terms that means one thing to believers and another to the unsaved?"

Sol answered curtly, "It is Biblical, is it not?"

Cady noted that angels seemed to have a very different sense of humor. "Your work, does it involve me today?"

"It does, and will each day until the Master calls you home," Sol answered solemnly.

Cady absorbed that, wanting to ask the pregnant question but did not. "When you disappear, where do you go?" Cady asked.

"Go?" Sol repeated. "Where do I go? I don't go anywhere. Where would I go?"

"I mean, sometimes I can see you, other times not, are you still there all the time?" Cady tried to clarify the question.

"Of course, always," Sol said. "You are my personal business."

"And others?" Cady continued. "Are there others who are your personal business?"

"Yes, indeed there are many."

"Can you explain then how you can be with all of us all the time? Isn't God the only one able to be omnipresent?"

Sol considered the question. "Yes, it is as you have said. The Father is everywhere all of the time. I am not."

Cady gasped, nearly leaving the road.

Sol was juggling several colored balls while sitting in the other seat, seemingly impressed with his own skill. Sol smiled the smile of an angel then said, "You are the red one. I am with you am I not? But also with the green, yellow and blue."

Cady was just beginning to get it when they crossed the bridge into the borough and Sol disappeared.

He parked at the 23rd and went inside where the desk sergeant handed him two message slips. One was from John and the other from Hissim. After roll call he sought out Hissim, finally finding him in the commander's office where he was waved in. Hissim had begun reporting but started over for Cady.

"Word in the Muslim community is that Allah will be glorified within the next 24 hours," he said. "Most have no idea what that really means, but I think it gives us the time line we were looking for."

Although there was no hard evidence, the watch commander was on the phone with the chief before they left the room. The chief in turn had the commissioner's ear within minutes.

When Cady returned John's call, John's voice was filled with excitement. "We intercepted a fake copier delivery late last night full of C-4 with a remote detonator. The place is swarming with sniffers and feds from the foundation to the roof."

Cady listened then filled his friend in on Hissim's latest information. "It's real isn't it?" Cady said sadly.

"Yes, my friend, I'm afraid it is," John answered.

The commander soon called the whole shift back into the briefing room and closed the door.

"Men," he said, "a few of you knew, some of you guessed, and many have no idea what has been going on behind the scenes for the past two months. The secrecy was necessary to prevent the perps from going underground and popping up when we were less prepared. We have a real and imminent terrorist threat aimed at the East Coast and possibly targets in New York City. We have intercepted several shipments of explosives and made arrests in concert with the FBI. Last night an attempt was made to deliver C-4 to the towers disguised as a copy machine."

"From the commissioner's lips comes the order that no one is to share this information outside of this room. If you feel the need to send your family for an unscheduled visit to Grandma in Kansas, do it. But do it without filling in any details that could be shared with friends. A panic in the city would kill more than the terrorists ever could. Be vigilant, use your instincts, use your heads, and if necessary your weapons. Search and seizure rules have been loosened a little to give you room to operate, but be smart about it. Wear your vests, cover each other's backs, and err on the side of caution. I am asking you to give us an extra four hours a day, doubling up with the next shift by starting four hours early. Beginning tomorrow, you'll work eight to eight with your relief coming on at four o'clock and working through to four in the morning. Needless to say all leaves, vacations, and days off are suspended until we get through this."

"Anyone have anything to add?" the commander asked.

Cady waited to see who might be forthcoming. "I have been involved twice and can tell you they have no fear whatsoever of dying. The usual threat of being shot is not a deterrent. Do not hesitate if faced with a choice."

"Well said," agreed Hissim. "The radical Muslim embraces death as a victory."

Cady took the wheel and Red rode shotgun. Neither had much to say for the first part of the morning. At coffee, Cady called home to let Shawna know he'd be working early tomorrow and his leave had been canceled. Gratefully she asked no questions. Red called Sarah begging off from their scheduled breakfast the next morning telling her only that he had been asked to work. She started to say that all court proceedings had been canceled and were being rescheduled for later dates but heard only the dial tone.

During what would have been their lunchtime, Cady and Red took a 10-32, man with a gun call, asking 10-18 response. It was a distraught man who had been served with divorce papers at work seeing suicide as a way out. The special response unit responded and eventually talked him down without shots fired.

A real break came at just after two o'clock when an undercover escaped a man with a knife in the Muslim district. The man was later taken into custody. The slasher was potentially off the street.

The first shift of double cover began at four with the eight o'clock guys arriving four hours early to provide extra visibility to the public and extra sets of fresh eyes on the streets. It was hastily decided that those who shared patrol cars would do the hand-off as usual while the retiring squad would patrol on foot at selected locations for the remainder of their shift. Cady and Red chose the World Trade Center specifically because John was there. Others were at the UN building, Statue of Liberty, courthouses, public buildings and on Wall Street.

Cady used his cell to call home. He asked Shawna to notify Ben of the unexpected change in plans and to give his regrets that he would not be available as planned. He cautioned her to not give specifics or too much information that might somehow become public knowledge.

He pulled into the driveway after nine, spent, tired to the bone, and weary of worry. Shawna must have given the girls a heads up because they greeted him and retired to their rooms to finish their schoolwork without their usual good-humored banter. Shawna poured him a cold beer in a frosty A&W root beer mug laughing as she did so. Just the kindness of the simple act touched him deeply and cheered him up. She had waited to grill his steak until she heard his car leave the pavement rather than warming it up. While it cooked she joined him at the kitchen table sipping occasionally from his mug. Slowly the cares of the day fell from his shoulders, but his heart remained heavy with dread.

Her white teeth were framed by her bronze skin and her dark eyes sparkled as she said, "See anything of Sol today?"

Cady laughed as he remembered. "Not since this morning when he rode to work with me." Then he related their conversation in detail taking special pleasure in describing the juggling act.

Shawna laughed until she cried. "Cady my old war horse, I think you have lost it. Your imaginary friend belongs in a circus not in heaven."

He ate with relish but declined her offer to take a horseback ride. He opted for a hot shower instead.

Cady was already in bed when the phone rang. It was Ben.

"Sorry to wake you old man," he said. "I've had to take a hopper out of Newark in the morning so the family voted to stay home. Maybe we can get together Thanksgiving or Christmas if our lives slow down a little."

Cady thanked him for the call and returned to bed but could not sleep. At five o'clock he was up and drinking coffee in the kitchen. When the family joined him the girls were still in their pajamas and planning to skip school. They were jacked about seeing Ben and his family until Cady broke the news to them.

The girls had already adopted a vacation mindset and complained that it was too late to get ready and go to school. Cady and Shawna smiled at them knowing there still remained plenty of time to make it to school. Cady allowed them to stay home with their mother, who had no intention of working either. Cady, however, was already dressed, so he left early for the city and his extended shift.

Eleven

Sol appeared as before but rode along quietly.

"Good morning my friend," Cady said. "It's nice to have your company this morning."

Sol smiled.

"Today is going to be a long day, I didn't much sleep. I might need you to help keep me on my toes," Cady added.

"Long day?" Sol mused. "Aren't they each the same, as you mortals count them?"

Cady shook his head. "I am surprised that you haven't picked up more understanding as to what we mean when we speak. We often speak in parables."

Sol contemplated what he heard. "A long day and keeping on your toes is a parable? Its meaning escapes me."

Cady laughed. "A long day means that time seems to move slowly making the day seem longer that it actually is. On my toes means to be prepared and ready for what happens."

"Oh, why then did you not just say that," Sol asked.

Cady shook his head again. "Why did Jesus speak in parables?" he asked his favorite angel.

Sol looked confused, hesitated, then answered, "It is not for such as I to ask or know."

Cady continued, "But He did, didn't He? And He always has a purpose, doesn't He?"

Sol nodded, looking stricken.

"We men, or mortals as you refer to us, often find God's Word as difficult to understand as you find my speech. We spend a great deal of time studying, guessing, praying, and asking for clarification of its meaning, do we not?" asked Cady.

"You do," Sol agreed.

"So then, my blond friend, why do you suppose He chooses to make it difficult for us to understand?"

Sol looked at him as though he had just committed blasphemy, but offered no conclusion.

"Let me offer you my humble opinion," Cady began. "He wants us to understand Him to work at digging out the deeper meaning of things, to begin to think in His terms. He doesn't make it easy because He wants our commitment and our desire to be deep and lasting, not superficial. Man remembers the lessons that come with difficulty and sometimes pain."

Sol was nodding, smiling once again. "Interesting," he said. "The Master has said that He has made you higher than the angels. I always wondered what that meant. And if so, how we could guide you?"

Cady suddenly turned serious and asked point blank, "Do you know the future?"

Sol looked at him for several seconds and replied, "Sometimes we are given advanced knowledge of events so that we may use that knowledge to guide our charges."

"Can you read my mind?"

"I am unclear. I do not fully understand what you are asking."

"I am asking if you know what I am thinking right now before I say it," Cady said with a little edge in his voice.

"Often, but not always," Sol answered with sincerity. "It comes more as a perception than actual knowledge."

"What then do you perceive that I want to know from you?" Cady asked.

"You want to know what I cannot tell you, what only the Father knows. When you will die."

"Right!" Cady said. "I am concerned about my family and about the time I will have with them."

Sol smiled. "Fear not, you'll have all eternity with them. That I know and can say with certainty."

They reached the bridge and were entering the city. Cady felt relief having confirmed knowledge of their salvation but still carried the feeling of impending doom. Sol was gone when he stepped from his car and waived to Red in the parking garage at 7:10.

Inside the 23rd, some of both shifts were present causing traffic jams and bottlenecks in the limited space. The beat cops got their assignments then joined their brothers on the streets. The patrol division struggled to hand off their vehicles and take up positions at the various locations presumed as targets. Faces lined with fatigue and worry replaced the normal more jovial ones as the eight o'clock shift began.

In the car, Red took the wheel and Cady grabbed his cell phone and dialed John's number.

"Bad time, brother, got about a million people arriving for work," John said hurriedly. "I'll call you back later."

Cady could imagine a few hundred security staff trying to screen several thousand rude, busy workers eager to get to their jobs on time. Overhead the day was clear with the weather promising to be warm and seasonal. Over his shoulder Cady caught a glimpse of Sol in his periphery. Sol sat in the rear seat center, just like a perp, with a look of seriousness on his radiant face.

Cady turned to Red, "See anything in the mirror?

"Just traffic," he answered, looking out the side window.

"No, in the other," Cady said, motioning to the rear view inside.

Red turned white and his mouth dropped open. "You can see him too?"

Cady was taken a back. "Too? You mean you can see Sol?"

Red pulled to the curb, obviously shaken. "Sol? Who is Sol? What I see is Thomas, an angel who has been with me lately. I thought I was going crazy when no one else could see him."

Cady looked again but saw only Sol.

"Let's get this straight," Red said. "You see someone in the back seat named Sol but no one called Thomas?"

"True as blue," Cady said, repeating a cop term. "Have you spoken to Thomas?"

"Yes, several times," Red said, regaining his composure. "And you?"

"Yeah, Sol and I visited all the way into the city this morning," Cady admitted.

"Wow!" Red exclaimed. "What do you think this all means?"

"Sol said he was a messenger and guide," Cady confided. "And that he is here to help me make decisions that will honor God and complete His plan."

It was 8:20 when a squawk came over the radio from dispatch. A 10-89, bomb threat, had been received at the courthouse. Several units responded 10-18. Red and Cady resumed patrol while filling each other in on their angel experiences as they drove. After Cady shared the cookies and milk experience, Red glanced into the mirror at Thomas who looked distraught but said nothing. Red wondered if angels experienced jealousy.

"When did you first see Thomas?" Cady asked his partner.

Red thought, and said, "I guess it was when I was a boy. I lived with my grandparents after my folks divorced. I was 12 when my grandma died and he was there in the room with me then. I saw him off and on for a while afterward and then not for years, until the day of the taxi bomb. I never told anyone, kind of came to think my mind was playing tricks on me."

"Do you talk with him?" Cady probed." How did you know his name?'

"Some," Red answered, "mostly not out loud, just in my head for the most part, until last week. He began to talk out loud where I could hear him. He told me he was called Thomas. What do you make of it, Cady?"

Cady took a deep breath before answering. "I have been wondering that myself but can't seem to get a specific answer from Sol. But given that his visits have become more and more frequent and our conversations more meaningful, I am guessing it may have something to do with this terrorist thing we have been involved in and our part in it."

"Spooky," was the young man's reply. "I was thinking that myself just this morning when he rode to work with me."

Cady looked again but saw neither angel. He turned to Red and asked, "See Thomas?"

"Nope, he's gone. He had dinner with us last night," Red added almost as an afterthought. "I asked Sarah to marry me."

"And?" Cady said smiling.

"And, she said, 'Yes.' We're looking at sometime around Thanksgiving. I was going to tell you today and ask you to be my best man," he continued.

Cady was elated. "Congratulations," he said with sincerity. "I'd be honored. Just let me know when."

They pulled to the curb and helped an elderly man push his car out of the intersection where it had stalled. They then proceeded downtown. Cady's cell phone rang. It was Shawna telling him she and the girls were having lunch with Helen.

When he shared the news about Red and Sarah, she came right back with, "I knew it! I saw it right from the first night. They were made for each other. We'll have to have to invite them out and hear all about it."

Cady concurred. "Sounds like a plan. Maybe next weekend, depending on how these extended shift hours work out."

~

John was on the phone, having taken a break after the initial rush of people. Although the traffic in and out was heavy all day and part of the night, the big hit came every day between seven and eight o'clock.

Cady started to relate Red's big news when John exclaimed, "May God help us! An airliner has just hit the north tower, near the top. Gotta go."

Almost simultaneously a squawk from dispatch confirmed what John had said. Within seconds every available unit was 10-18, en route, to the World Trade Center.

When they arrived four minutes later, the great tower was billowing smoke and flames three-fourths of the way up. Debris and glass were falling, and people were running and screaming everywhere. Several black and whites had already arrived, and one ambulance was at the near curb. In the distance sirens wailed from approaching emergency vehicles as word spread of the tragedy in progress. Many victims just sat down in shock with unseeing eyes, and they were bombarded with falling remnants of the plane and building. Cady and Red rushed to move them across the street and out of harm's way as backup and fire trucks arrived. It was 8:42 when Cady entered with several other officers attempting to restore order and evacuate the wounded giant. Pandemonium reigned in the foyer, but as they made their way up the stairwell they found offices where people were still at work, ignoring entreaties to evacuate. Cady remembered the building to be in excess of 100 stories. With elevators shut down automatically, the trip down from the upper floors was brutal for those who chose to leave. He hoped a contingency plan would provide evacuation from the roof via helicopters for those on the floors above the crash. Cady and Red climbed fifteen flights before ushering survivors down the stairway.

Cady's cell phone rang. It was John on the 44th floor looking for information about medical personnel. He was with two seriously injured and one with a heart condition, who was unable to negotiate the stairs. Cady promised to relay that information to command and get back to him.

An explosion rocked the mammoth structure making it sway like a wounded prizefighter. Reports from the ground confirmed that a second plane had struck the south tower at 9:03, at its midpoint, nearly ruling out the possibility of an accident. Cady knew at once the event that they had worked to prevent was in progress. Turning his charge over to the troops on the ground he inquired about med-assist on the 44th floor and was told they were already on their way up. Cady called John but received no answer. As he began the slow climb a second time Red was nowhere in sight. He thumbed his mic only to find communications overloaded and unavailable.

A small group of firemen used their keys to enable one of the many elevators in an attempt to evaluate feasibility of their limited use. The human-caused noise level was deafening with bullhorns, sirens and machinery adding to the clamor. At the 20th floor Cady was forced to stop and catch his breath. When he tried his phone again John answered.

"On the way down," John panted into the phone. "Just passing the 24th floor now with two vics and 15 ambulatory."

Cady came back, "I'm on 20 headed up to meet you."

En route his phone rang. It was Shawna who had seen the events on breaking news television. Cady confirmed what he knew, that he was not injured, but was headed up to help John evacuate survivors.

"Pray for us?" he asked before hanging up.

At the 22nd floor he met John who was leading a ragged band of evacuees followed by four firemen carrying a man down in a basket. Behind them two EMTs were aiding a bandaged man and woman to walk.

Cady stopped the firemen and asked, "Any chance of using the elevators for the wounded?"

Grimly the lead man shook his head. "We have been advised of possible explosive charges in them. Command has curtailed their use for the time being."

"Where can I help?" asked Cady, having caught his breath. Without waiting for an answer he took a young red-faced fireman's place on the basket. "Take a break," he said as they moved downward.

This scenario repeated itself every five floors or so, as one man would relieve another. By the time they broke out into the foyer all of them were spent, gladly giving up their charges to waiting hands. New crews of men passed them, retracing their steps as they rehydrated and rested a few scant minutes.

Cady could see the south tower clearly. It appeared to be canted slightly, the weight of the upper floors pushing downward on the damaged floors below them. Red moved up beside him, looking much older than his years, with tears running down his cheeks. Cady handed him a water bottle. Wanting to join Red in his misery Cady restrained himself.

Cady struggled to his feet and tried to smile before asking, "Seen Thomas? We could use some help here."

Red smiled wanly. "Nope, I haven't. I expect he's real busy here too."

John looked pasty white when he passed Cady. Whether from strain or simply from the horror of the event, Cady could not tell.

A sea of flashing lights on emergency vehicles filled the streets as far as one could see. Grim men, eyes filled with pain, entered and re-entered the two smoking giants. Their steps became forced and mechanical as their bodies began to weaken. Above them the north tower continued to burn with black smoke billowing into the almost cloudless sky.

~

At Newark International, Ben retracted the landing gear of UA Flight 93 scheduled non-stop to San Francisco International and settled into the cockpit for a routine flight. He had a crew of six and 37 passengers on board. Just as they left Pennsylvania he heard a disturbance outside the cockpit. That he sent his co-pilot to investigate became a fatal mistake. As the door opened the co-pilot was overpowered, and four men forced their way into the cockpit. Before he had time to react, Ben felt his life's blood flowing from his body as a hijacker passed a box cutter across his throat. His last thoughts were of his wife and children. He died with a prayer on his lips. He was immediately replaced by one of his attackers, who turned the plane back eastward toward a new destination.

Passengers who had cell phone communications received information of the attacks on the twin towers and immediately knew their intended fate. Knowing that survival was not an option they chose rather to force the plane down in a rural area where other lives would not be lost. Those able to do so rushed the cockpit and overpowered the hijackers. The plane ran into the ground in a field in Pennsylvania. Forty-four, including the four terrorists, died.

Unknown to Cady, UA Flight 77 had also been hijacked and was successful in an assault upon the Pentagon. Many brave and loyal Americans were killed.

At approximately ten o'clock the unimaginable happened. The weakened support structure in the south tower gave way and the building collapsed. Hundreds of people were killed or trapped and unable to escape, including many first responders. Crews went into rescue mode rushing to the twisted, smoking, rubble-strewn heap, formerly a shining example of man's engineering prowess.

Red, Cady and John remained in the north tower and worked feverishly in the rescue effort alongside their selfless brothers. In just over an hour they had climbed the grim stairways three times, returning each time with injured, disheartened and terrified souls. At about 10:15 John collapsed near the 5th floor unable to breathe. Cady and Red carried him down to ground level where he was left with the paramedics like any other victim in cardiac distress.

As they reached the 15th floor the smoke became unbearable. Fewer and fewer were finding their way down. Firefighters with oxygen pushed by them hoping to find more survivors. They advised Cady and Red to suit up or leave.

Cady called home but got no answer so he left a message on the recorder. Next he tried Helen. Her line was busy. Red borrowed the phone to call Sarah but got a recording so he left a message.

They were on the 9th floor headed down with three survivors when Sol appeared to Cady.

Red stopped in his tracks, stared at the blank wall before him and said, "Thomas, is that you?"

"No," answered Cady, "that's Sol."

"But I can see him too. It must be Thomas," Red insisted.

Their voices were as one as the two angels addressed their charges. "Can you remember what our Master said to the thief hanging on the cross beside Him?"

Immediately both Cady and Red were given clear recollection of Luke chapter 23 verse 43: "And Jesus said to him, 'Assuredly, I say to you, today you will be with Me in Paradise.'"

At 10:28 the north tower fell, killing most and trapping many in the rubble. Darkness overcame them. It became impossible to breathe, as his body shut down. Cady's mind turned to another time and place beyond recognition. Sol held his hand and walked with him into the Lord's presence.

Epilogue

The world knows of the tragedy, but only those closest to it have the lifelong connection to it. Phil was forced to raise her children alone. Kate offered her help and support. John survived for a time, but several years later succumbed to the cumulative effects of heart disease and cancer caused by the incident, leaving Helen alone. Red died without having children, or enjoying a full life with Sarah. Sarah never did marry, choosing her career over other suitors. Bernie lived to see her sons graduate from college. Thomas became a career officer in the Air Force, and Ted became a physician with a wife and three children. Joe and Bill are still best friends and live in New York. Joe is a proud member of NYPD's finest, and Bill is a state patrolman. Both are married with children and are active in their church. Judge Baines retired early and is working as a counselor for troubled youths. Shawna and her three children returned to Idaho where she works among the native tribes as an advocate. Faith became an Olympic hopeful in downhill skiing before being injured in the finals. The twins, Hope and Charity, graduated college with honors, moved to Texas, and received doctorates at the Dallas seminary.

AUTHOR'S NOTE

Apparently the rubble and debris of the Twin Towers were not sufficient to give our hero eternal rest. Like an old bear coming out of hibernation for a final season, Cady Miller returns with our old friends and some new ones to serve God yet again in his own unique way. It was my original intention to write just two Cady Miller books using the 9/11 tragedy to close out the saga, but as He often does, God seems to have had another plan. This third and final book is Shield of Justice, which begins with Cady trying to retire and enjoy his remaining years with Shawna. Instead he finds himself drawn into a drama of real-life tragedy.

Matthew 27:51-53, "Then, behold, the veil of the temple was torn in two from top to bottom; and the earth quaked, and the rocks were split, and the graves were opened; and many bodies of the saints who had fallen asleep were raised; and coming out of the graves after His resurrection, they went into the holy city and appeared to many." We read in Hebrews 9:27-27, "And as it is appointed for men to die once, but after this the judgment, so Christ was offered once to bear the sins of many." NKJ.

Cady, among others mentioned above, is an immortal and continues to walk on earth among us, doing the Lord's will at prescribed times and places until Jesus returns. He appears without memory of the past and without knowledge of his own special place in God's plan.

ABOUT THE AUTHOR

A native Idahoan, Danney Clark is recently retired after a forty-year career in the insurance industry. For the past five years he found time to write and publish several novels, short stories and poems. A devoted husband, father and grandfather, he enjoys God's great out of doors in many venues including hunting, fishing and camping. Writing is his passion, and God is his mentor. He is pleased to offer his considerably varied works for others to enjoy. The first book in this series, Shield of Faith, has been well received and has several very positive reviews. Please sample his shorter works from the library on his Web page at www.danneyclark.com.

28197213R00104

Made in the USA
Charleston, SC
04 April 2014